STAY A LITTLE LONGER

KAIT NOLAN

Stay A Little Longer

Written and published by Kait Nolan

Cover design by Lori Jackson

Copyright 2019 Kait Nolan

AUTHOR'S NOTE: The following is a work of fiction. All people, places, and events are purely products of the author's imagination. Any resemblance to actual people, places, or events is entirely coincidental.

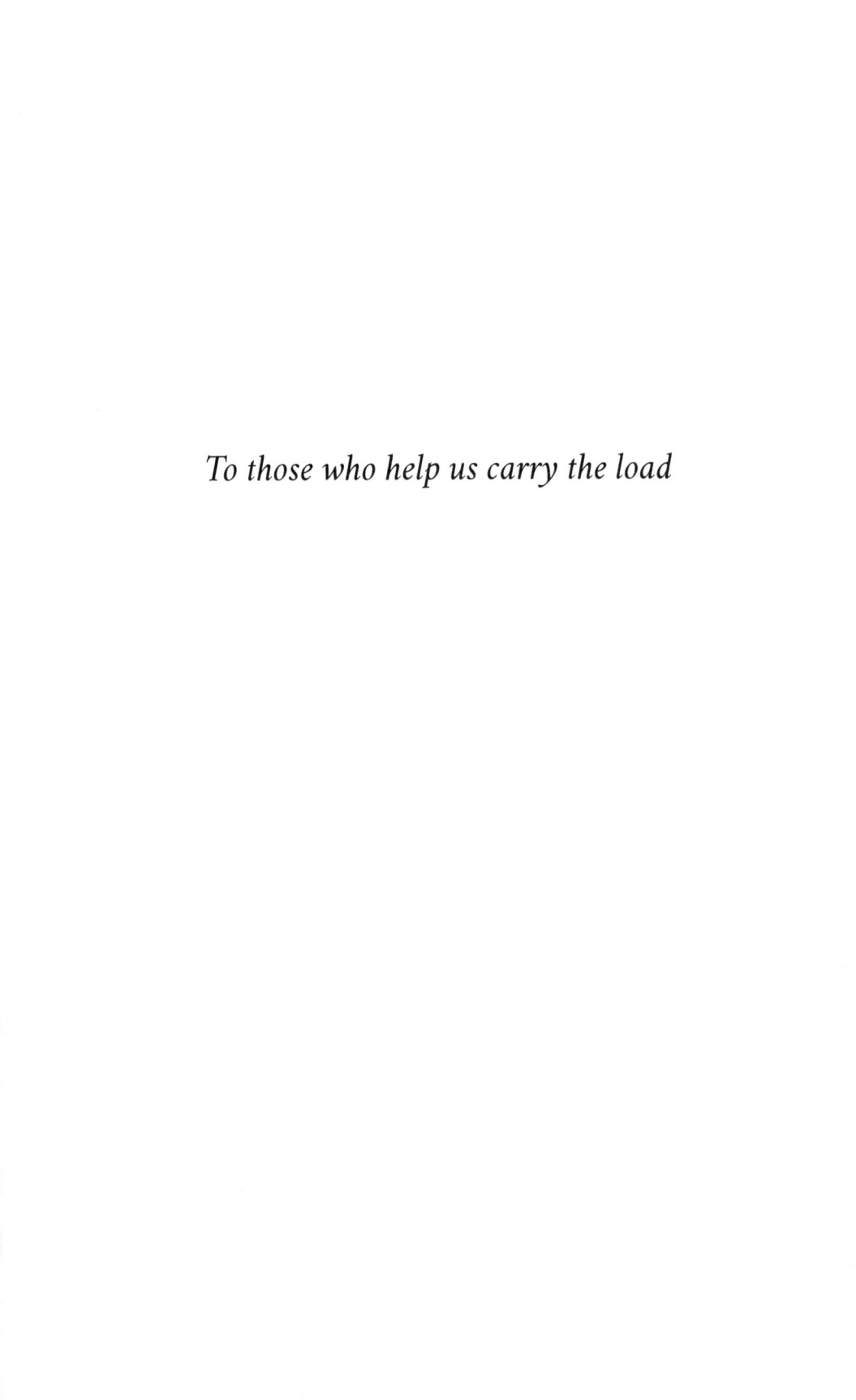

To those who help us carry the load

A LETTER TO READERS

Dear Reader,

This book is set in the Deep South. As such, it contains a great deal of colorful, colloquial, and occasionally grammatically incorrect language. This is a deliberate choice on my part as an author to most accurately represent the region where I have lived my entire life. This book also contains swearing and pre-marital sex between the lead couple, as those things are part of the realistic lives of characters of this generation, and of many of my readers.

If any of these things are not your cup of

tea, please consider that you may not be the right audience for this book. There are scores of other books out there that are written with you in mind. In fact, I've got a list of some of my favorite authors who write on the sweeter side on my website at https://kaitnolan.com/on-the-sweeter-side/

If you choose to stick with me, I hope you enjoy!

Happy reading!

Kait

CHAPTER 1

"The port syrup and pear were simply an exquisite pairing with the Hudson Valley foie gras. But my favorite...my favorite was the ricotta and chard ravioli with the garlic cream sauce."

Chef Athena Reynolds listened as the man with the balding pate and paunch hanging over his belt continued to gush about her food, praising the flavor combinations and hypothesizing about her inspiration and influences as the meal itself turned cold and the carefully perfected sauce began to congeal. A muscle ticked in her jaw at the travesty unfolding before her. She wanted to simply turn and stalk back into her kitchen. She despised this part of the job. The food should speak for itself. She shouldn't have to. But the investors who'd made her dream of opening her own restaurant a reality insisted that she trot out like a show pony to shake hands, smile, and be gracious. That was far more her oldest sister Pru's natural inclination. She was the nice one, who'd played peacemaker among their ragtag collection of foster siblings. Athena was...well...her talents lay elsewhere, usually managing sharp things—from her favorite knives to her tongue—with alacrity. She could filet this douchecanoe with just a few, choice words...

But the voice of Jayson Straker—her boyfriend and one of the powers that be—rolled through the back of her mind.

You'll catch more flies with honey than with your acerbic wit.

It was easier to take that kind of criticism while lingering in bed after excellent orgasms than it was to hear it from any of the *other* owners. Almost everything about working at Olympus had gotten easier since Jayson bought out one of her original investors. He believed in being on-site and involved in the day-to-day running of things. She'd fought him at first. Fighting was what Athena did best, next to cooking. But it turned out that they shared a vision—one that would capitalize on her James Beard win and the Michelin star she'd earned and catapult them both into the stratosphere of the foodie world. She just had to be patient and make it through this round of ass kissing without maiming or insulting the guy so she could get back to her natural habitat.

"And those glazed cipollini onions with the merlot reduction."

It's a cabernet reduction, you asshat. Athena started to say just that and stopped herself.

The nicer you play, the more customers come, and the closer you are to being able to buy out a controlling share in Olympus.

That was her ultimate goal. One she'd expected to be closer to achieving by now. But there had been complications and expenses and other necessary diversions of those funds. And then there was the fact that she hadn't been able to create anything new in months. She'd been skating by with the help of her well-trained kitchen staff and her sterling reputation as a chef. But that would only take her so far. So here she was, standing in the dining room in the middle of a mad dinner service, listening to this pretentious asshat wax rhapsodic, as if he knew a damned thing about her food, when he didn't seem to grasp the essential point that it should be eaten when it was served. At the perfect temperature. So help her, if he completed this indignity by pulling out his phone to immortalize the now ruined meal on Instagram, she was coming after him with her chef's knife.

"I simply can't wait for the chocolate soufflé. I'm sure the spiced plum sauce will be simply inspired! Though surely peach would be better."

The smile Athena had fixed on at the start of his recitation felt brittle as glass. She hoped it didn't come off as the grimace it really was. "Well, that's certainly—" She searched for something positive to say. "—a well-considered opinion. I appreciate your patronage of Olympus." Before he could do more than open his mouth to speak again, she rushed on. "I'm so sorry, but I need to be getting back to the kitchen."

Without waiting for a response, she fled. With luck, Jayson hadn't noticed that part of the exchange. He'd fuss. And if he did, she'd just cook him something that would shut him up. He always forgot everything else when he ate her food.

Back at the pass, she expected a pileup of plates waiting for her final inspection before being carted out to the dining room by servers. But there were only two dishes under the warmer. A quick glance at the carousel showed way too many tickets still waiting to be started.

"Where the hell is the steak for table seventeen? There should be three quails waiting to go out. And the scallops for table nine. And what about the lamb for table two?"

"Waiting on the entrees, Chef." The brisk response came from Poppy Woolicott, one of her line chefs.

This was a disaster. The dining room was an absolute madhouse tonight. They couldn't afford to be backed up.

Athena rounded toward the grill to lambast her sous chef for falling down on the job. But Mari wasn't at her station.

"Where the fuck is Mari?" she demanded.

Moses Lindsey, her tattooed badass of a pastry chef, jerked his head toward the back stairs. "She rushed out of the kitchen a little after you headed out to the dining room."

"In the middle of service?" Athena's voice was quiet, measured. Deadly.

"She looked a little green. Like she maybe got some bad takeout." This came from Cory Oliver, the newbie on her staff who'd graduated from dishwasher to making stock just two weeks before.

For just a moment, Athena closed her eyes and drew in a long breath, focusing on the sounds of running water, simmering pots, and sizzling skillets. A warrior preparing for battle. Then she was flying, moving through the kitchen toward the grill, shouting orders that had her staff jumping as if the sirens had just blared to warn of an impending airstrike. Which they had. As soon as they got through this mess, someone's ass was getting smoked.

It had been ages since she'd been on the line herself. The unfortunate reality of the job was the head chef did little of the actual day-to-day cooking, but rather spent her time as a general coordinating the army and checking the quality of everything leaving the kitchen. Running the world was far more her sister Maggie's purview, but Athena could sure as hell run her little piece of it. Still, she'd missed the actual preparation, the juggling of cooking multiple dishes and seeing them all to perfection. She lost herself in the rhythm of it, in the scents and sounds of the food. The harsh edge of frustration and the constantly simmering anger began to dull. This was her therapy. Her bliss. In this little corner of her universe, she controlled all.

By the time they hit a few minutes' lull, Mari still hadn't returned to her station. Mariana Grafton never dropped the ball. It was what made her an invaluable member of the team. One of the primary reasons Olympus was a success. She was a damned good sous chef. Second in command. She'd never bail in the middle of service unless something was horribly wrong. So because she was family—because everyone who worked in Athena's kitchen eventually became family if they stayed long enough—worry edged out the anger as Athena went hunting for her friend.

"Moses, keep an eye on things."

"You got it, Chef."

She headed first to the bathroom down the hall from the kitchen, but the door hung open, the little room dark. The alley out back was likewise empty. Back inside, Athena jogged down the narrow stairs that led to the basement, which housed their wine cave and the offices. Not that Athena used the glorified closet assigned to her. But Jayson's office, where he managed the financial side of things, was down here. It was where they usually shared a nightcap and deconstructed each service to decide what had gone well, what could be done better. It was also the only room outside the bar that had a landline, as Athena refused to have a phone interrupting the sanctity of her kitchen and forbade cell phones during service.

His door was closed. Beyond it she could hear the faint murmur of voices, then a sound like crying. Alarm cut through what remained of Athena's temper. Was it Mari's father? She knew he hadn't been doing well these past couple of months. Mari had worried he'd been pushing himself too hard, that he was going to have a heart attack or a stroke. She'd been an absolute rock when Athena's mother had died last year, picking up the slack when Athena had been almost too broken to function. Athena would sure as hell return the favor.

She opened the door. The words of support died on her tongue as she took in the scene on the other side. Mari sat on Jayson's desk in her chef's coat, her pants dangling to the floor from one ankle, her head thrown back. Jayson stood between her legs, his own pants around his knees, the ass Athena had always so admired flexed as he froze, right in the midst of driving into her sous chef.

For one stunning moment, Athena couldn't breathe. There were too many betrayals to process. Not only were her boyfriend and the woman she believed to be her best friend having an affair, they were doing it all but under her nose, in the middle of service, in the restaurant they'd all worked and slaved to make the best. The fragile trust she so rarely gave cracked under the weight of this new reality, and from the faultline poured rage.

"What the actual *fuck?*"

"Athena, I can explain," Jayson began.

"Really? You think there's any sort of explanation I'll accept for how your dick happened to fall into my sous chef? Stay the hell away from me." Athena rounded on Mari. "And you, don't you dare step foot back in my kitchen. You're fired."

Mari made some sound of protest, but Athena was already turning, already rushing back upstairs as the two of them fumbled to put their clothes back on.

She couldn't afford to lose her shit. Tonight was a full house. There were a myriad of important guests. But the fury built in her chest, so scorching hot and bright, she wondered smoke didn't pour out of her nostrils like a dragon. Her staff paused for half a second when she reappeared.

"You all have work to do!" she barked.

No one said a word. They just leapt back into motion as she crossed to the carousel and yanked down the next ticket. Poppy knew better than to interrupt when Athena elbowed her out of place and began to dice the vegetables herself. This wasn't how things were done, but she didn't give a good damn. This was *her* kitchen. *Her* world. She needed to find some control over *something* right this minute or the heat in her chest was going to go nuclear. So she diced onions with vicious speed and precision, her favorite Damascus steel knife a comfort in her hand.

He'd cheated on her. That was bad enough. But she realized Jayson had sent her out to schmooze with that pompous prick to *get her out of the way* so he could have a quickie with her *best friend*—or maybe not so much of a quickie given they were still going at it when she'd found them. And they'd done it *here*. In her restaurant. Her haven. Her dream. The image of the two of them was burned into her retinas. The arch of Mari's neck. The straining muscles of his arms as he gripped her hips and—

"Athena." Jayson's voice sounded pained.

She didn't think, didn't even hesitate before she whirled and hurled the knife. Someone screamed. Jayson dove to the floor, seconds before the wickedly sharp blade dug into the wall, an inch from where his head had been.

"You bastard," she snarled. "Get the fuck out of my kitchen."

"Are you crazy?" he demanded, rolling to his knees and staring at her as if he'd never seen her before.

"I'll show you crazy, you lying, cheating son of a bitch!" She grabbed up another knife.

Jayson lunged for a huge, stainless-steel bowl full of greens, holding it up as a shield and spilling salad everywhere as she advanced on him.

And then her feet were flailing as big, strong arms wrapped around her from behind, lifting her off the ground. "Drop the knife, Chef." Moses's thick rumble of a voice came at her ear.

"Let me go!"

"Not until you drop the knife. You can beat his ass with your fists if you want, but the knife ups the charge. You don't wanna go where they'd send you for that, whether he deserves it or not," Moses murmured. "Drop it, Athena, before you do something you'll regret."

She'd already done so many things she regretted. What was one more?

But she did as he ordered, opening her hand and listening as the blade clattered to the floor. Moses set her down, hesitating before releasing her. Her breath sawed in and out like a bellows as she stared at her former lover and realized he'd permanently tainted what was hers. So there was grief boiling up beneath the anger as she fisted her hands and retaliated in the only way she had left.

"I quit. Good luck running Olympus without me."

"HE's GORGEOUS! Those big brown eyes and all that glossy red hair." Ari Reynolds-Bohannon pressed both hands to her heart and fell back against the front seat of the truck with a gusty and dramatic sigh. "I'm in love."

Logan Maxwell suppressed a sigh of his own, grateful the girl was talking about the latest gelding to be added to his stable instead of Sebastian, his new stable master. At fourteen, that could go either way. Better he encourage the horse crazy over the boy crazy. "Chestnut. That coat color is called chestnut."

"Chestnut," Ari repeated.

Logan's muscles ached, reminding him he'd been in the fields since dawn and awake with livestock an hour before that. Spring planting was in full swing around the farm, and his days were filling up. But he'd been carving out time to teach Ari to ride in exchange for her help around the barn with the horses. She had the makings of a good little equestrian, and he got a kick out of her enthusiasm. So he dug up a grin as she continued to chatter on about the horse's many virtues.

"He's gonna need a barn name, you know. Think you can come up with one?"

"Me? Really?"

"Sure." If the animal worked out like he

hoped, he'd be Ari's new mount. Not that he was telling her that yet.

"That'd be *awesome!* I'll make a list."

Of course she would. He chuckled. "You do that."

"Can I come out again tomorrow?"

"That's something I wanted to talk to you about. You know we're about to be hitting the real busy season around the farm. I'm gonna be tied up a lot more as we get closer to harvest."

Ari's face fell. "Oh. Well, I understand. Maybe we can pick back up in the fall?"

That instant acceptance of disappointment just killed him. A former foster kid, Ari had been adopted just before Christmas by his friend Pru and her husband, Flynn. They were a devoted, stable family, who'd gone through hell to make sure the girl didn't get sent back into the system after the death of her foster mother —Pru's own mom, Joan, who'd been taking in foster kids for twenty-five years. Not for the first time, Logan wondered what Ari's life had been like before she came into the Reynolds family.

"No, that's not what I meant. I was thinking, if it's okay with your parents, you could maybe spend a little more time at the farm this summer. Take a bit more responsibility with the horses."

The teenager's eyes went round. "Really? What about Sebastian?"

The ex-Army ranger was technically the one in charge of the horses. Which was to say, he lived in a little cabin on the farm and managed the daily feeding, care, and training of the half-dozen rescue animals Logan had somehow acquired simply because there'd been a need and he had an empty barn. But that number would probably be rising soon, and they'd need more able bodies to do all the work.

"He could use a hand, and mine will be full. You've proved yourself capable and a quick learner."

Ari clasped her hands and widened those big brown eyes in an expression that reminded

Logan of his baby sister, Laurel. "Will you come in and talk to Mom and Dad about it? Please?"

He really hadn't had the time to drive all the way into Eden's Ridge to drop her off. The tractor had crapped out again, and if he didn't get the damned thing running for tomorrow, he wouldn't get the north field plowed and the broccoli seedlings in the ground before the rain hit this weekend. He'd had enough trouble working around the extra wet spring to get seedlings planted. But Pru had texted that something had come up and begged. Since riding lessons for Ari had been his idea in the first place, here they were, piled in his truck and nearly to her house. If he went in, he'd get drawn into a visit because that's how life went in the south. But hell if he could resist that face. He needed a break anyway. It was getting on toward dinner time, and he was optimistic enough to hope he'd score an invite so he didn't have to scrounge for his own supper tonight. Cooking took energy he didn't have.

"Yeah, all right."

"Yes!" She pumped her fist and he swallowed his chuckle. This kid was a trip.

The late April sun still rode high, slanting through the trees to dapple the big Victorian house that Pru and her sisters had turned into a bed and breakfast last year. The Misfit Inn nestled among the trees, perched on top of a bluff overlooking the Great Smoky Mountains. Off to one side, work trucks surrounded the converted barn that now housed the day spa. He wasn't sure exactly what they were doing over there, but the Reynolds sisters were nothing if not ambitious.

Parking in the circular drive, Logan climbed out of the truck, trailing Ari up the steps and following her through the front door without preamble. She made a beeline for the kitchen, toward the babble of voices that made it clear the gang was all here. He wondered if he was inadvertently interrupting a family meeting.

"Athena!" Ari's joyful squeal had Logan's step faltering.

But it was too late to hide. He'd already made it to the doorway.

The sight of her was a sucker punch, as it always was. Even with lines of fatigue bracketing her eyes—typical after the full day of travel it usually took her to get here from Chicago—she was the female equivalent of a shot of top shelf tequila. Her long brown hair was caught back in a tail that trailed over one shoulder. The mouth he was used to seeing curled in a sardonic smile bowed up as Ari grabbed her in an enthusiastic hug, but she didn't quite pull it off. There was something, some chink in her usual armor that had his curiosity piqued. Athena wasn't one to show weakness of any kind, and it had him wondering what that vulnerability was about.

Athena wrinkled her nose. "You smell like horse."

"That's because I've been grooming them all afternoon." Beaming, Ari swung around. "Look who's here, Logan!"

Athena's gaze snapped up, catching sight of

him in the doorway. In an instant, she pokered up. "Hey Logan."

"Hey."

Everybody started greeting him at once, but he was only half paying attention because Athena's gray eyes were still on him and he couldn't look away. Unbidden, his mind went to her sister Kennedy's wedding last summer, when he'd met those eyes across the crowded reception. Her smile then had been flirtatious and playful, and the tension between them had been thick enough to strum, even from twenty feet away. Giving in to that electric need had led to the best night of his life. But that was all it had been. One night. And a handful of phone calls that made them...not quite friends but more than a simple wedding hookup. It had ended there, in that liminal space. Her life was in Chicago and by the time he'd seen her again at Christmas, she'd been attached to someone else, so his longing for a repeat performance had come to nothing. And that was for the best. He didn't have time for...anything.

But as he stood at the edge of the big kitchen, with several of her family members and the big farmhouse table between them, he realized the electricity was still there, humming between them. He wished he'd taken the time for more than just changing out of his muddy boots before coming over here.

"Didn't expect to see you here." *Logan Maxwell. Farmer and master of understatement.*

If Athena was as affected as he, she didn't show it. "The restaurant is under renovation, and I've got some time off, so I drove home with the idea that I'd help out with the inn. With Pru getting close to her third trimester, I didn't figure y'all would turn down some extra hands."

Pru rubbed a hand over her pronounced baby bump. "You are not wrong."

"How long can you stay?" Ari demanded, draping an arm around her shoulders.

In the beat of hesitation, as she wrapped an arm around her niece's waist, Logan saw Athena reach for something other than the truth. "Not sure, exactly. At least a couple of weeks. Probably longer. Renovations are so uncertain."

"You've got that right," Pru agreed. "You probably saw all the trucks. Porter's been trying to work on the expansion for the spa around appointment times, and it's driving me absolutely batty."

As conversation turned to construction issues, Logan wondered about the lengthy stay and whether Athena's boyfriend had likewise chosen to come to Tennessee during the renovation. He had something to do with Olympus, right? There was no sign of him in the kitchen, no other luggage piled in the corner but her single suitcase. What did that mean? Was he still in the picture? It wasn't like he could ask in front of this audience.

"—stay for dinner?"

Logan blinked, realizing Pru was talking to him and he hadn't been paying a damned bit of attention. "Sorry?"

"You should stay for dinner."

"Xander will be here," Kennedy added, referring to her husband and Logan's best friend.

"Do stick around and help me balance out all the estrogen," Flynn added. Pru shot her husband a mock glare, to which the Irishman responded with a smacking kiss and a spate of Gaelic that had her cheeks going pink.

For a moment, Logan considered it. He'd come hoping for food, and if he stayed, he might actually find out what he wanted to know. But what purpose would that serve? Even if Athena was single again, she'd never give up Olympus and he'd never give up his land. There'd be no picking up where they left off that hot summer night. And that was for the best because he wouldn't want to stop with just one more taste. So better to let that attraction fade with time and distance.

"I really can't. I've got a date with a recalcitrant tractor."

Ari's lip instantly rolled out in a pout.

Logan couldn't stop himself from glancing at Athena to see her reaction. Not disappointment. Not relief. Maybe the pull was one-sided after all this time.

The weight of Pru's speculative gaze made him want to twitch. Through circumstances he didn't quite know the details of, she knew about his night with Athena. She'd kept the secret as a bit of quid pro quo because of the shenanigans she'd gotten up to with Flynn that night and had said no more about it. But he knew she thought of it every time he and Athena were in the same room.

Ignoring the look, Logan focused on the reason he'd come inside in the first place. "I really just stopped in to ask if it'd be okay if Ari did some more work on the farm this summer, with the horses. If you can spare her from the inn, that is."

"Please, Mom? Please, please, please, please, *pleeeeeeease?*"

"It'd be minimum wage and more riding lessons for payment."

"I'd get *paid?*" Those eyes lit up again. "This just gets better and better."

"We'll talk about it," Pru promised.

Logan just nodded and took a step back. "I'm gonna leave y'all to visit. I need to get on back to work." He was already turning away, as he looked back at Athena. "Welcome home."

She inclined her head. "It was good to see you, Logan."

Was it?

He told himself again that it didn't matter as he lifted his hand in a wave and walked away. But he knew he'd be puzzling over the mystery of Athena Reynolds the whole time he fought with that damned tractor.

CHAPTER 2

hen Jayson's number flashed up on the screen of her cell phone, Athena almost smiled. Not even twenty-four hours in Tennessee. He hadn't wasted time getting to the groveling, and she appreciated that. Not that it would be anywhere near enough to make her accept whatever bullshit explanation he intended to offer for his cheating, but abject supplication would go a long way toward mollifying her temper in the absence of actual bloodshed. Which she owed Moses a thank you for preventing.

"What do you want?"

"Don't hang up. Please. We have things to discuss."

She gritted her teeth at the sound of his voice, her empty fingers clenching for the knife that wasn't there. "I don't think I'm much in the mood for discussion."

"I'm sorry for how things went down."

"You're sorry you got caught, you mean."

He heaved a sigh, and she could just imagine him pinching the bridge of that blade-straight nose. "Athena, I'm trying to apologize."

"There is no 'I'm sorry' big enough to make up for what you did. If you think you're going to weasel your way back into my bed, you've got another thing coming."

"I'm not calling for that."

She opened her mouth. Closed it again. She didn't want him back. She hadn't been in love with Jayson so much as the idea of him. Of a man who shared her passion for food, her vision for the future. It wasn't heartbreak she was wrestling with but sheer, unmitigated fury at her own stupidity for trusting him in the first place. Still, him not begging her to take him back was a blow to her pride.

"Then why are you calling?"

"About Olympus."

Ah, here was what she really wanted. Him imploring her to come back to take her rightful place in the kitchen. That was what really mattered in all of this.

"I want to buy out your share in the restaurant."

Her brain staggered and stopped. She hadn't heard that right. For a full ten seconds she sat on her bed, mouth agape as she tried to figure out what he'd really said.

"Athena, are you there?"

"You...what?"

"I think we can both agree after how things ended that working together will be impossible. You made the right decision in leaving, so I want to buy out your share. You'll be free and clear to do your own thing."

Which really meant, *I'll be free to put the chef*

of my choosing in your place. She was under no delusion that it would be anyone other than her backstabbing bitch of a sous chef.

The tide of fresh betrayal rolled over her like a tsunami, knocking her off whatever even keel she'd managed to cobble together since she'd left Chicago.

Had they *planned* this? Had the two of them played her? Known her well enough to predict that she'd fly off the handle and quit her own restaurant in retaliation for the affair? The very idea of it had her blood boiling.

"Do you have any idea how insulting that is?" She snarled the words, wishing for something sharper that would do more damage. "Olympus is mine, Jayson. My vision. My dream. My fucking Michelin star. It isn't Olympus without me."

"You are, unquestionably, the creative mind behind the menu and the concepts. But the recipes belong to the restaurant, and you don't own the controlling share. I do."

Of course he'd throw that back in her face.

The truth of it scalded her. She shoved up from the bed to pace. "You bastard."

"I'm trying to do the right thing here, Athena. I'll make you a generous offer for your portion." He named a figure that had her brows climbing to her hairline. "I know you need the money."

And that was just another betrayal. She'd cared for him, confided in him. He knew the reason she hadn't been able to buy up more shares in the restaurant than she had. And damn him for using that against her.

Damn him for being right.

But if she did this, if she handed her baby over to him, to them, she wouldn't just be severing professional ties. She'd be lacing that bridge with C-4 and blowing it to kingdom come.

She tried to imagine going back to Chicago, back to Olympus. Tried to imagine some sudden windfall that would allow her to turn the tables and buy that controlling share from *him*. And she knew almost at once that she couldn't do it. He'd poisoned the whole place for her. She'd never again be able to cook in that kitchen without imagining them there. Without remembering the pain and the fury and wanting to stab him all over again.

She let out a slow, controlled breath. "Fine. I'll sell you my share." Thinking about Maggie's blood-thirsty negotiation tactics, she shot a figure back at him that was a good thirty percent higher than what he'd already quoted her. He'd probably say no, but she might as well try to get in one last lick on him.

"Done. I'll have the paperwork drawn up and sent to you as soon as possible."

Staggered by his ready agreement, she could only stare at the wall.

Jayson's tone went soft. "You're a brilliant chef, Athena. I wish you all the best."

Before she could snarl back an appropriately scathing reply, he'd hung up.

She dropped the phone onto her bed before she could hurl it at the wall. It was over. The dream she'd fought for tooth and nail, sweated blood and tears to make a reality, was gone. On some level she'd known that when she walked out, and it hadn't stopped her. The hurt, the anger, was too huge to stop her from throwing it away because escape had been more important. Now she had no job, no source of income to take care of the responsibilities that hung around her neck like a noose.

What had she done?

Panic and grief welled up, tightening her throat, making her eyes burn.

No. Fuck this. She hadn't cried at her mother's funeral. She wasn't going to cry about this. Tears were senseless. A waste of hydration and energy. But she needed to do *something* to let all of this out.

In less than a minute, she was searching through kitchen cabinets and drawers, taking stock of the contents of the refrigerator and freezer. She needed comfort food. Not merely the soothing deliciousness of carbs and fat but the act of creating it. She needed to prove that something in her world still made sense.

Ari came in, Kennedy behind her, as she piled ingredients on the big island.

The girl dumped her backpack in one corner. "Ooo, you're cooking! What's on the menu?"

"Shepherd's pie." Because it had been Mom's favorite and being back in this house where she'd spent her teenage years made her ache to curl up at Joan's feet and ball yarn as she spilled out the whole sorry mess and waited for her adoptive mother's unique brand of wisdom to make her feel better. But she'd never get the chance for that again.

"I love shepherd's pie. Can I help?"

Before she could come up with a response that wasn't a growl, Kennedy swung an arm around Ari's shoulders. "Athena's pretty territorial about her kitchen space. She doesn't like anybody underfoot."

"I can follow directions," Ari insisted.

Athena wanted to say no. She wanted to be alone. Wanted the chance to *actually* cook, preparing a meal herself from beginning to end, with no waiting patrons, no stakeholders, no prospective critics, no snooty-ass foodie wannabes putting in their two cents. There'd been no opportunity for that in months. But looking at the open enthusiasm and gangly limbs of her niece as she folded herself onto a stool at the counter, Athena couldn't bring herself to snap at the girl. This upset wasn't about her and she didn't deserve to bear the brunt of Athena's shitty coping skills.

"You know how to brown ground beef?"

Ari grinned and brought her hand to her brow in a sharp salute. "Aye, Captain!"

Despite the simmering rage, Athena's lip twitched. "The correct response is 'Yes, Chef.'"

As Ari slid off her stool and came around to pull out a skillet, Kennedy lifted her brows in surprise. Of everyone in the family, she was the only one Athena had ever trusted in the kitchen.

After a moment's hesitation, she jerked her shoulders. "You wanna prep the mushrooms?"

Kennedy's smile spread slow. "Yes, Chef."

35

This, too, was a Thing. She hadn't cooked with Kennedy in years. She'd barely spoken to her sister to spew anything other than accusations about how Kennedy had selfishly left all of them behind when she turned eighteen and stayed away a full decade. When Kennedy had returned to Eden's Ridge for Mom's funeral, it had been...bad. Still reeling from the loss, Athena had needed a punching bag, and Kennedy had been a prime target. But the situation hadn't been what they'd all believed. Her reasons for leaving hadn't been selfish. And over the past year, Athena found she'd finally let go of the resentment she'd been toting around.

As Kennedy moved smoothly around her, she felt some of the tension in her shoulders ease. This felt familiar. Good.

At the opposite side of the island, her sister began cleaning the baby Bella mushrooms. "This feels like old times."

Athena glanced up, her knife not slowing as she efficiently cubed the potatoes she'd scrubbed. "Nah. There'd have to be Verdi playing at ear-splitting volume and Lorenzo constantly trying to pinch our asses."

"I do not miss that man."

"Who was Lorenzo?" Ari asked.

"Lorenzo Ossani is one of the most lecherous, temperamental chefs to ever walk the streets of Florence, Italy. He's also a freaking god of food. Kennedy and I spent a memorable summer sweating it out in his kitchen, learning everything he'd teach us. The stuff I learned from him was the reason I got into Le Cordon Bleu."

"That was the last time we cooked together," Kennedy murmured.

A band squeezed around Athena's chest as she thought of the years they'd lost. No going back to change things. They only had the now. She swallowed against a knot in her throat. "I've missed this."

"Me, too."

The click of a camera had them both turning to look at Ari, who shrugged, unrepentant. "I had to capture that Hallmark Moment." She shoved her phone back into her pocket. "Now tell me more about your adventures in Italy."

Athena scraped potatoes into the pot of boiling water on the stove and checked the progress of the meat. "Mind what you're doing. Break those big clumps up into something smaller with the back of your wooden spoon, and see that you get the surface brown but not burned. That's the Maillard reaction and where all the flavor is."

"Yes, Chef."

Returning to her cutting board, Athena started on an onion. "So there was this guy we called Meatball..."

"You missed an *awesome* dinner the other night. Athena made these veal and shiitake meatballs and Mom had to stop me from going back for a third helping."

As Ari circled the paddock on the new gelding, whom she'd dubbed Ridley, Logan marveled at the girl's ability to continue chattering while she rode. "Heels down," he reminded. "Don't let those reins droop."

She made the corrections and kept talking, going on and on about the food until his stomach growled.

"It's been so great having Athena in town for longer than a couple of days at a stretch."

Logan hadn't seen Athena since the day she'd arrived a week ago. Spring planting had been a convenient excuse to stick close to home. It wasn't that he didn't want to see her. It was that he couldn't see her and not want to get involved. She was off-limits. He didn't poach in another guy's territory. And that aside, whatever issue she was dealing with would tug at him, at his insatiable curiosity, until he got emotionally involved wanting to help. Because you could take the therapist out of the master's program, but you couldn't take the training and instincts away. He'd learned his lesson on that front years before. So he'd stayed away for both their sakes.

Still, he couldn't quite resist pumping Ari for a little more information. "Step it up to a posting trot. You've been spending a lot of time with her on this trip?"

She bounced a little before settling into a smooth rise and fall with the gelding's gait. "She's been teaching me to cook!"

"Really? I thought she defended the sanctity of her kitchen with all those sharp knives."

"That's what Kennedy said, too. But she's turning me into a proper sous chef. Yesterday, I made béchamel sauce. She says it's one of the five primary sauces in French cooking."

"Yeah? What did you do with it?"

"Made a killer mac and cheese. Like, seriously, to die for. You should've been there for that, too."

Amused, he propped a foot on the bottom rail of the paddock fence. "What's with all the dinner invites all of the sudden?"

"Oh, I don't know. Maybe I'm feeling sorry

for you in your bachelor state, with all the boxed mac and cheese and beanie weenies."

"I'll have you know, I have not eaten beanie weenies since I got out of college. Change directions." Not that his bank account was a whole lot healthier now. Everything he had was sunk into this farm. He'd finally obtained his certification as organic. Now he began the never-ending battle to keep it and sell enough of his crops to cover the outlay to get there, which hadn't been chump change. Oh, and pray that his equipment held out for at least one more season. Some of it was presently being held together with baling wire, duct tape, and prayers. So maybe the kid had the right idea to mooch meals when he could manage it.

Ari shot him a pitying glance as she smoothly executed the transition. "Please. I've seen the state of your kitchen. Hungry Man meals do not constitute actual food."

They did when you'd put in a fourteen-hour day and didn't have the energy to do more than push a few buttons before falling face first into bed to do it all over again tomorrow. "Is that you or Athena talking?"

"Does it matter? It's the truth either way. Besides, we have an award-winning chef at the house right now. Why wouldn't you want to enjoy that as much as humanly possible?"

He had a sudden flash of long, tanned limbs wrapped around his shoulders and hips. Shaking his head to dislodge the image, he cleared his throat. "Because I've been busy with planting, as we've already discussed."

"All the more reason to join us for dinner, so you don't have to cook."

He didn't point out that joining them for dinner would involve quitting his work day early in order to shower and make himself presentable, not to mention drive time both ways and the lengthy socializing involved with a Reynolds family gathering. Not that he didn't enjoy her family, but he legitimately didn't have that kind of time.

"Besides, you're all into the organic farming

thing. Athena's into high-quality ingredients. You've got food in common."

"Pretty sure everybody with taste buds and a stomach has food in common. Step it up to a canter."

Instead of nudging Ridley's flank, she continued the conversation. "You know what I mean. Y'all can talk about ingredients at a higher level than the rest of us."

He narrowed his eyes at her. "Are you trying to play matchmaker?"

Her grin was a challenge. "So what if I am?"

"Her boyfriend would probably have a problem with it."

"He's not here. And anyway, I don't know if they're still together. She hasn't mentioned him. I mean, wouldn't you mention the love of your life to your family?"

"He may not be the love of her life." *Please don't be the love of her life.* "That doesn't mean he's not still in the picture."

Ari waved that off. "He shouldn't be in the picture. We've never even met him. Besides, you like her. And whether he's still around or not, the two of you have chemistry."

"And how would you know that?" Surely Pru hadn't said anything...

"Please. I have eyes. Besides, I've been surrounded by couples making googly eyes, with little cartoon birdies flying around their heads, for a year. The inn might as well be called The Love Shack."

Logan snickered, imagining Xander's pained expression if he heard this exchange. "I feel confident in saying that Athena has never made googly eyes in her life."

"You're not denying the chemistry," Ari pointed out.

"Ari—"

"I'm just saying maybe, if we give her enough reasons, she'll decide to stay."

As an adopted kid, Ari was thirsty for family. She was happiest when all of hers was in Eden's Ridge. It was sweet, and he appreciated that she saw him as a check in the "Reasons Athena Should Stay" column. But he needed to nip this idea in the bud. Not only to protect her but to squash that tiny flare of hope that had lit in his own chest.

"I hate to burst your bubble, kid, but Athena's life isn't here. Once the renovations are done, she'll be headed on back to Chicago, to Olympus. That world, that life, isn't compatible with ours." It was as much a reminder to himself as to Ari.

"Athena's not happy in that world," she insisted.

"How do you know that?"

"People talk about the things that make them happy. She's hardly said two words about Olympus since she got here. And if you ask, she finds a way to change the subject."

He hummed a noncommittal note, but he thought back to her evasion about how long she was staying. Was something more serious going on back in Chicago? Had something besides fatigue carved those lines around her eyes?

Not your business.

"Anyway, she's not happy, so maybe she should walk away."

"That's easier said than done. She's one of the best in her field, and she deserves the chance to shine."

"Of course she does, but the sun does not rise and set in Chicago. She could shine closer to home."

"That's for Athena to decide. Now step it up to that canter."

This time Ari did as he asked. But as she slipped smoothly into rhythm with her mount, Logan couldn't help but wish that the teenager was right.

CHAPTER 3

*A*thena had put this trip off for more than a week. Every single time, it got harder and harder to make herself go. Guilt inevitably got her over the hump and forced her into the car for the forty-minute drive to the campus just south of Johnson City.

The grounds of Haven Acres were beautiful. Long, grassy lawns, studded with trees that had leafed out for spring, gave way to stunning views of the mountains. That was part of why she'd chosen it. It wasn't quite the view he'd had at home, but it was a damned sight better than the endless stretches of institutional beige and cinderblock walls of the state facility he'd been in for years before she'd made enough money to get him out. Not that he usually seemed to notice one way or the other, but maybe, somewhere down deep, he could feel the change.

She stopped in at the front desk of the nursing home's main building to find out where he was this afternoon.

"Miss Reynolds! It's so good to see you again. We didn't expect you back so soon."

Athena forced a smile, though she thought it might break her face. "Neither did I."

As the woman checked the schedule on her computer, she kept up a steady stream of small talk. Somehow Athena made appropriate responses, though she wouldn't have been able to say what they'd talked about on pain of death. The receptionist gave her directions, and Athena murmured her thanks.

Heading out the back door of the main building, she crossed the wide lawn, which was flanked on two sides by more buildings, creating a sort of quad that opened on the fourth side to the mountains. Beyond the buildings, various groups were clustered outside, enjoying the sunshine of a gorgeous spring day. To the south, a knot of people went through the slow, stylized movements of Tai Chi. Further up a small rise, half a dozen others had easels set up.

Away from all of them, a wheelchair was parked beside a bench, beneath a redbud tree that had burst into bloom. Its occupant faced the mountains, a light blanket tucked across his lap. A nurse sat on the bench, a paperback in hand, reading glasses sliding down the bridge of her nose. As Athena got closer, she could hear the woman reading aloud.

"There waiting, silent and still in the space before the Gate, sat Gandalf upon Shadowfax: Shadowfax who alone among the free horses of the earth endured the terror, unmoving, steadfast as a graven image in Rath Dínen."

Athena recognized it as *Return of the King*, one of his favorites. She had to pause for a minute, closing her eyes to find some control. It had been so many years since she'd heard him read it himself. So many years since she'd heard him speak at all. She couldn't quite remember the sound of his rich, rolling voice anymore, and that was just another loss on top of so many. Another layer of herself flayed away by the whip of fate. Every visit left more scars on her heart.

When she was certain she could keep herself together, she crossed the rest of the way and crouched in front of the wheelchair. "Hey, Daddy."

There was nothing in the gray eyes so like her own. No flicker of recognition. No acknowledgment he even knew she was there. A bad day, then. Bracing herself for that, she turned and introduced herself to the nurse.

"How's he doing?"

"Physically, he's perfectly healthy. He's still not usually responsive to people, but he recognizes food when it's put in front of him. The occupational therapist has been working with him on relearning how to feed himself. There's been some progress with that." The nurse smiled. "Won't acknowledge a vegetable, but he almost always reaches for pie. He's got quite the sweet tooth."

Athena swallowed. "Yeah. He always has. Do you mind giving us a little bit?"

"Of course." She handed the book to Athena and left them alone.

After a moment's hesitation, Athena sank down on the bench and looked out at the view. She wondered if her father saw it, or if he saw something else wherever he was trapped inside his own mind.

"So, I've got news. I sold my share in Olympus. The paperwork came in day before yesterday." Before she could change her mind and do something radical like burn the contracts, she'd signed them and overnighted them back, wanting the whole thing over and done with. "I got a good offer on it and the money's all clear and in my account already."

Her fingers restlessly stroked the edges of the paperback. "It's a big change. I've still got to make a plan and figure out what's next. Probably it's gonna mean leaving Chicago and my apartment there. Not that that's any great loss. I barely spent any time there other than to sleep. But all that can wait a little bit. I need some time to grieve."

She paused, waiting for some change in body language. He didn't even shift in his chair, so she kept talking. "I haven't told my sisters yet. The reasons why I did it are...ugly and embarrassing. I made a bad decision. Seems I've made plenty of those over the years. But I wanted to make sure you knew you're taken care of. The money from the sale will cover us both at least through the end of the year. By then I'll have figured something else out."

She reached out to take one of his hands in hers. His fingers were soft. Weak. Not the strong, callused hands she'd known as a child, when he'd been the one to hold everything together. That was her job now. Had been her job far earlier than it ever should have been. She clenched her teeth, all but snarling the promise. "I'm always going to take care of you."

But there was still no response. His fingers didn't tighten in hers. He didn't move or look away from the view. So she squashed her disappointment and released his hand, picking up the book. "Let's see what Gandalf is up to."

She read until her voice gave out, waiting for some sign of life, some indication he wasn't just a shell. But there was nothing. When she couldn't take it anymore, she waved the nurse back, thanked her and hurried to the parking lot.

Safely ensconced in her car, she folded both arms over the steering wheel and pressed her face tight against them, her throat so tight, she thought she'd strangle on the urge to cry. When would she give up? When would she stop hoping, stop expecting that he'd fight his way out of the prison of his mind to give her some sign he even knew she was there? When would she acknowledge that her father had died in all but body years ago?

Unable to cope with the threat of tears, she reached for the anger that always battled them back. Because this hadn't been an accident. This nightmare had been her father's own fault, and she'd been paying and paying and paying for his mistake for years. The familiar heat of rage was cleansing, if not comforting. She was beyond comfort at this point.

Her phone dinged with a text. Straightening, she took a half dozen measured breaths before digging it out of her purse and thumbing open the screen. She found a message from Moses.

Duck and cover.

There was a link to something on YouTube.

Frowning, she loaded the video. As soon as it filled her screen, her fingers tightened on the phone.

"Oh shit."

To Athena's mind, some disasters unequivocally merited getting shit-faced. As it happened, there were only two places to get drunk in Eden's Ridge. Elvira's Tavern catered to the respectable crowd, the nice folks who rarely indulged enough to start a bar fight. As it was also where Kennedy worked as a bartender, and as Athena had absolutely no intention of talking this shit out with her sisters, it was automatically off the table.

That left The Right Attitude. She'd always privately thought that meant a bad attitude, given the clientele who frequented it. Those respectable folks didn't darken its door, and the Sheriff's Department was on speed dial. Heads were regularly cracked and glassware busted. She hadn't been inside since an unfortunate incident testing out a fake ID when she was eighteen, but best as she could tell, the place hadn't changed much. The squat, cinderblock building was a dingier shade of brown than it had been eight years before. As she came through the door, she noted the decor had been upgraded. Dozens of brassieres stood sentry around the perimeter of the room. Not just any bras, but buxom, over-the-shoulder boulder holders, in a blinding display of pattern and color.

Classy.

For a moment, she stood in the entrance, waiting for her eyes to adjust to the dim light. The air was hazy, despite the non-smoking ordinance in town, and the floors seemed to suck at her feet as she made her way over to the bar. Aware of the eyes following her progress, she kept her gait loose and ignored them, dialing in her best fuck-with-me-and-die face. Which wasn't hard, considering the reason she was here.

The bartender, a rangy man who could've been anywhere from mid-forties to mid-sixties, wandered over. His steel gray brows shot up as she slid onto a stool. "You in the right place, honey?" His voice was gravel and his face was dominated by a mustache that was a way-less-attractive homage to Sam Elliot.

"I'll give you a hundred bucks for a bottle of Jack, a clean glass, and no questions."

He inclined his head and slapped a glass on

the scarred wooden bar in front of her. Snagging the iconic black-labeled bottle, he set that in front of her, too, then waited. Clearly she was expected to pay up on the front end. Fine. She dug a hundred dollar bill out of her purse and passed it over.

In the back of her mind, Maggie's voice chided her that this whole thing was a foolish indulgence. She poured two fingers of whiskey into the glass and downed it in one, fast shot. The real Maggie would have plenty to say later. Athena sure as shit wasn't going to be lectured right now. She deserved this one night to fall the hell apart and mourn the torpedoing of her career.

Someone had filmed her confrontation with Jayson. Someone on her staff, someone she'd made a part of her work family, had recorded the whole damned thing. It hadn't been clear from the position of the camera who it had been. They'd sat on it until the final paperwork had been signed, sealed, and delivered. Until she was no longer connected to

Olympus—and couldn't do anything to retaliate.

But it had already gone viral, racking up four hundred thousand views since yesterday.

Jesus.

She poured more whiskey, knocking it back just as quickly and relishing the burn down her throat and into her chest. It complemented the fresh rage that had been simmering there since she'd seen the video.

Someone leaned against the bar between her stool and the next. "You lookin' to forget something, sugar?"

She poured more whiskey. "If you don't want me to take that pool stick and shove it up your ass, you will walk away right now."

"Aw now, don't be like that."

Slowly, she turned her head to look at the guy. He wore a white cowboy hat. It was the only pristine thing about him. Two or three days' scruff dusted his angular jaw, and some kind of dark grime rimmed his nails. Grease probably. A guy who worked with his hands.

Under other circumstances, she might have been into that. She appreciated a working man —even more so after the flagrant betrayal from her white-collar ex. But tonight she was feeling mean. Or meaner than usual.

Something of her mood must've shown in her expression because the flirtatious smile slid off his face and he backed away real slow, as if she were some kind of rabid animal.

Looked like he had a few brain cells after all.

Turning back to her whiskey, she sipped this one slower, going back to mulling her problem. Even if she had some kind of PR team who could act—and the idea that she'd have such a thing was laughable—there'd be no containing the video. That runaway train would keep on escalating because people loved drama, loved bad behavior.

Look at the chef who utterly lost her shit and tried to kill her boss.

Never mind that if she'd been trying to kill him, he'd be dead. Or that the whole thing had nothing to do with their professional relationship. That was the relationship the public at large actually knew about. They'd kept their personal ties quiet. It had seemed like a good idea at the time. But now...This would taint her professionally. No matter that she had a Michelin star or that she'd won the James Beard Rising Star Chef of the Year. No one would care about the truth of the situation. The reasons why.

This was a shitstorm of epic proportions.

It would fade. Eventually. But who would want to touch her after this? How was she going to support her father? Haven Acres was ungodly expensive. After finally getting him out of the crappy state facility he'd been languishing in, she couldn't bear to send him back. She didn't know how much he knew, how much he was aware of, and she wasn't ever going to risk him believing she didn't care or that he didn't matter. They'd both suffered enough of that from the woman who'd given birth to her.

The lone comfort in all of this was that the

sale of her share of Olympus gave her enough cushion that she could figure it out. She didn't have to rush and leap at the first option that presented itself. She'd be generous and assume *something* would come up. Optimism came easier as the level of amber liquid in the bottle dropped.

Unless something miraculously turned up in the next week or two, she'd have to tell her sisters something. That was a real pisser. They'd want her to talk about *feelings*. She'd rather scrape her knuckles across a microplane. What good did talking about that shit do? It didn't change anything. And God, she really didn't want to admit the truth of what happened with Jayson. So maybe…maybe she could come up with some half truth about why she'd decided to walk away. Right, because they'd believe her when she spontaneously walked away from her life-long dream for some *other* reason. She had time to figure that out, too.

The bottle of whiskey clattered against the lip of the glass as she poured herself another

shot. In the category of more immediate problems, how the hell was she going to get home?
Driving was off the table. Had been three shots
ago. She wasn't about to call the inn and worry
her very pregnant sister. That would lead to
those questions she didn't want to answer.
Same result if she called Flynn. Kennedy was
working, and her *other* brother-in-law was the
freaking Sheriff. That'd look just fabulous for
Xander to come rolling in to scrape her off the
floor here. Yeah, no.

There was really only one person she could
call. One person who wouldn't judge, wouldn't
lecture. Resigned, Athena pulled out her phone
and dialed while she still could.

CHAPTER 4

*L*ogan jolted awake to "Carry On Wayward Son." The book he'd been reading fell to the floor with a thud, and his border collies rose from their spots on the rug at his feet to give a pair of short, sharp barks, as if to say "We're ready, Dad."

Scrubbing a hand over his face, he grabbed for the phone skittering across the table and thumbed the screen to accept the call. "Hello?"

"Logan."

The sound of Athena's voice on the other end of the line had him straightening in the chair. "Hey." He wasn't about to tell her he'd been sleeping at—he checked his watch—nine-thirty. She'd probably saved him from a kink in his back.

"I nnneed a faaaavor." Her words were slurred, and he could hear the faint sound of voices and indistinct music in the background. Was she drunk dialing him?

"Yeah? What's that?"

"Need a ride."

He bit back the myriad of questions he wanted to ask and zeroed in on the most important. "Where are you?"

"The Right Attitude."

He went brows up. That place was pretty rough. What the hell was she doing there? "Don't go anywhere. I'm on my way."

He left the dogs home, much to their disappointment. By the time he got to the bar, he'd considered and rejected a dozen scenarios for what was going on. She'd either tell him or she wouldn't. His best guess was this either had something to do with her family or she didn't want them to know about whatever it was she'd decided to drown in alcohol. Why else would she call him?

He didn't see a car he recognized, but then he had no idea what she drove. Either way, that was a problem for tomorrow. Inside, he spotted her almost at once. She sat at the bar, a semi-circle of space around her as the other patrons gave her a wide berth. Her hair was down, curtaining her face, and she swayed a bit on her stool. As he neared and caught sight of the mostly empty fifth of whiskey, he understood why.

Knowing she was a woman who struck first and asked questions later, he didn't touch her, instead leaning into her field of vision. The moment he caught sight of the unfettered grief on her face he wanted to gather her into his arms.

Oh baby, what happened?

But he kept his hands to himself. "Athena."

At the sound of his voice, she turned toward him and her expression of misery faded. "Llllogan. You came."

"Said I would. You ready?"

She glanced down at the last inch of alcohol in the bottle and frowned. "I'm not finished."

"I'm thinking you're gonna regret tomorrow enough without finishing that off. How 'bout you come with me?"

She squinted at him. "Are we going swimming? You were fun to swim with."

A blast of arousal shot through him at the suggestion. Under other circumstances, he'd have given damned near anything to go back to Opal Springs and get naked with her. But she was three sheets to the wind and hurting. "I think it's still a mite cold for swimming."

"Too bad." She finished off the whiskey in her glass and groped for the bottle.

He nudged it out of her reach. "I still think we ought to get out of here."

"I told you that last summer." Her lips curved, as if at the memory.

"Yeah, you did. It was a great idea."

"It really was. You look really good naked."

He couldn't stop the grin. "You look pretty amazing naked yourself."

"We should get naked again."

Yes, please.

"What about your boyfriend?"

Her face shut down with a scowl. "I kicked that cheating bastard to the...*hiccup*...curb."

So she was single again. Good to know. Not that he'd be doing anything about that tonight. "Good for you. Why don't you come with me? You can tell me about how you castrated him."

"Okay." She slid off the stool and would've kept on going until she hit the ground if he hadn't caught her.

"Whoa there. I've gotcha." Sliding an arm more firmly around her, he tried not to notice how good it felt to have her body plastered against his. A feat made harder by the fact that she rubbed her cheek against his chest like a cat.

The bartender eyed him up and down.

"She called me for a ride," Logan explained. "Is her tab settled?"

"Paaaaid up front," she slurred.

The bartender nodded confirmation.

"All right, then. Let's get you out of here." He scooped up the purse hanging on the back of her stool and headed for the door.

She took two, stumbling steps and sagged into him, giggling. "Shhh, don't tell Pru."

"Nope. We won't tell Pru." He'd take her home with him first and see about getting her sobered up some before driving her back to the inn.

As soon as he had her buckled into the passenger seat, he dashed a text off to Flynn, letting him know Athena was safe. Remembering what she'd said, he sent a follow up text asking him not to tell Pru. He didn't feel great asking the guy to lie to his wife, even by omission, but something about this whole thing pricked his therapist's need for discretion. Circling around, he slipped into the driver's seat.

She drooped against the door, pressing her cheek to the glass. "Shitty, shitty night. Shitty, shitty week."

He hoped like hell she didn't get sick in his truck. "Why's it shitty?"

"Fucking asshole was fucking my backstabbing sous chef."

He winced. "Ouch. That *is* shitty."

"That's not all. I blew it up."

"Blew what up?" He was reasonably sure she didn't mean a literal bomb.

"Everything."

"What's everything?"

She didn't answer, trailing a finger through the condensation of her breath against the window. Oh yeah, she was gonna be in hangover central tomorrow. And she'd be pissed if she thought he'd seen her vulnerable. So he lapsed into silence for the rest of the drive.

She was only semiconscious by the time they got back to the farm. Not trusting her to walk, he swung her up into his arms and carried her to the house. Her head lolled against his shoulder. He thought she'd passed out until her lips began to nibble their way up the column of his throat. The blood drained out of his head.

"Athena."

"You taste good."

With considerably less dexterity than he'd possessed a few minutes ago, he managed to get the door open and carried her inside. Water. Water and coffee and some preemptive painkillers. That was the plan.

As he came through the door, the dogs began to bark. Athena groaned at the noise, curling closer into him.

"Hush!" he ordered. They did as commanded, but still milled around his feet, sniffing at Athena as he crossed to the sofa. Very carefully, he lowered her.

She opened her eyes as he was trying to extricate his hands. "Logan." The low, sleepy rasp stoked his nerves.

"I'm gonna make you some coffee." If his words were choked, she wasn't likely to remember.

"Don't need coffee." Fisting her hands in his shirt, she yanked.

Already unbalanced, he tumbled onto her. Her arms locked around him and her mouth found his like a heat-seeking missile. His brain emptied of everything but the taste of her—whiskey and heat and woman. Potent and delicious. That flavor had haunted him for nearly a year.

She was a fever beneath him, her hands skating over his shoulders, across his chest, touching and taking and driving him mad as her mouth devoured his. He wanted this. Needed this. Needed her. Not until her hands fumbled with his belt buckle did he manage to come back to himself.

She was drunk off her ass. They couldn't do this.

With herculean effort, he managed to pull back, clamping his hands around her wrists to stop her from getting further than the half-un-buckled belt. "Stop."

"Want you."

"I want you, too. But not like this. You're drunk, Athena."

She pouted. It shouldn't have been sexy. "I can still help you get it up."

They both looked down at the erection straining his jeans. "I don't think that's in question. But you aren't thinking straight, and I'm not going to take advantage."

"Because you're a fucking gentleman."

"Yeah."

"Dying breed," she declared.

"Maybe so. I'm getting you water and making coffee." He managed to slip free of her grip and hurried to grab some water and Advil in the kitchen.

She had a dog on either side of her when he came back. "I'm seeing double."

"They're littermates. That's Bo and Peep."

She snickered. "Where's Little?"

"You'll have to ask my sister, Laurel. She named them as a joke. Here, take these."

She tossed back the painkillers and guzzled down the water. He waited a minute to see if it was going to stay down. When she didn't immediately throw it back up, he went back to start the coffee. As he moved around the kitchen, he could hear the incoherent monologue she directed at the dogs.

His jaw cracked on a yawn. He was gonna regret this whole thing tomorrow when he had to be up before the sun. But not nearly as much as she was going to regret it. Nearly an entire fifth of whiskey by herself. He shook his head.

By the time the coffee beeped, he'd gotten his arousal under control. "Hey Athena, how do you take your coffee?"

Not hearing a response, he headed back to the living room.

She was passed out on the sofa, one arm draped over Peep, with Bo curled in the crook of her legs.

He sighed. There'd be no getting her home tonight. She could sleep it off in the guest room. Shooing the dogs, he scooped her up again and carried her upstairs to bed.

A SCREAM DRAGGED Athena from sleep and into a world of pain. Her head wasn't attached to her body. That was the only possible explanation for why it hurt so damned bad. The scream came again, longer, louder this time, and she realized it wasn't a scream at all. It was a rooster crowing the dawn. The sound shot jagged shards of ice through her brain and had her curling into herself on a moan. Dawn meant it was way the hell too early to be up, and if that thing didn't shut up, she was going to wring its neck and turn it into a stew. She knew a thing or three about turning tough meat into something soft and succulent. Even if the idea of it made her stomach turn at the moment.

The cock crowed yet again and she wanted to rage at it, but that would require moving and making noise, neither of which she was capable of just now. And why was that? Struggling to swim through the ocean of throbbing in her skull, she tried to remember what had happened. Her mouth tasted as if something had crawled inside and built a nest, then died. But there was a faint undertone of something sweet and medicinal. Whiskey. She had dim memories of a bottle of Jack Daniels. Seemed like there'd been a lot of it, so maybe that had something to do with why she felt like death. But she was in the restaurant business. She knew how to hold her liquor. Except...no, she wasn't in the restaurant business anymore.

A fresh wave of agony rolled over her as everything came flooding back. Olympus. The video.

She whimpered.

The last thing she remembered was being somewhere around the halfway mark on that bottle of Jack. Where the hell was she?

Cracking her eyes, she squinted up at the ceiling. A motley assortment of glow-in-the-dark stars were scattered across it. She knew those stars, knew those faux constellations of The Waddler Penguin and Quackers the Duck.

She'd stared at them every morning of her life from the time she was six until she turned twelve. Frowning, she turned her head—regretting it at once—and caught sight of the built-in bookcase along one wall. The wall wasn't the right shade of pale purple but instead some warm neutral that glowed faintly with morning light. The furniture, including the bed she lay on, was different than she remembered. But this was her childhood bedroom. Which meant she was still dreaming. Of course she'd have a hangover in her actual dream. Because she couldn't get the blessing of oblivion like a normal person. And if the headache was this bad while she was unconscious, what would it be like when she surfaced?

Fighting through the ache, she dragged herself upright, bracing for the unsteady pitch and roll of her stomach. When she thought she could manage it, she stumbled toward the window to look out at her farm, at the home she'd been forced to vacate so many years ago. Except this wasn't her farm. Her farm had never looked all green and lush and gorgeous like this. But still, she recognized the barn, painted a cheery red, with crisp, white trim. Beyond it she could just see the first rows of the apple orchard where she'd spent hours climbing trees and reading. A wave of homesickness, stronger even than the hangover from hell, all but brought her to her knees. She didn't know which was crueler...that her dreaming mind should have brought her back here at all or that it should have made the place look like paradise.

It all looked so real. As if she could reach out and touch it. And suddenly, she wanted to do that with a desperation she hadn't felt since she'd been taken away from here as a child. She made her way downstairs, past the walls that should have held pictures documenting her childhood, and out the front door, into the breaking dawn. The air was still crisp and full of the scents of green, growing things and rich, freshly-turned earth. Birds twittered faintly and the rooster had finally shut up. Thank God. She clutched her elbows, hugging them close as she soaked up the sense of home. Not as she remembered, but as it should have been. It soothed some long raw wound in her soul.

From somewhere beyond the barn, a dog barked. Her heart leapt.

Sam?

But it wasn't her mutt racing from around the corner. It was a pair of border collies she didn't recognize. Neck and neck they raced toward her, sending up happy yips. It didn't even occur to her to brace herself, so when the dog in the lead jumped up, it knocked her flat on her ass.

"Ow!"

Somewhere between the stinging palms and the enthusiastic tongue bath to her face, she realized she was very much awake. Which meant...she really was on the farm where she'd grown up. Except her father had never been able to coax this kind of abundance from the land. How the hell had she gotten here?

Shoving back the dogs, she dragged herself

to her feet…and saw Logan's truck far out in the north field. Memory came back in pieces. She'd called and asked him for a ride and he'd brought her here? He had no way of knowing this had been her childhood home. Which meant…it was his. The farm that had claimed so much of her family's blood, sweat, and tears belonged to someone else. Someone who'd made of this place what her father never could. The idea of it sucker punched her already bruised heart. In her present state, she had no defenses, no walls, and this was more than she could take.

How could she face him after this? The truth was, she couldn't. She'd break.

I have to get out of here.

Stumbling in her haste, she went back into the house. Now that she was looking, she saw change everywhere. New paint. Refinished floors. Different furniture and art. Her house, but not her home. A sob threatened to erupt from her throat. She scrambled up the stairs, finding the water and painkillers on the bedside table this time. Downing them both, she rounded up her purse and shoved her feet into the shoes lined up neatly by a rocking chair in the corner.

How the hell was she going to get home? Her car was still at the bar. She didn't want to get into any of this shit with her sisters. Not yet. And she didn't want to wait for Logan to finish whatever early morning farm chores he was on. Thumbing through her phone, she called the one other person she knew wouldn't judge her right now.

"Porter, I need a favor." Her foster brother could always be counted on in a crisis.

"Athena? Everything okay? It's really damned early."

"Did I wake you?"

"No. I was about to be leaving for the job site at the spa to check on progress. What's the matter?"

"I need a ride to my car. I left it at the bar last night."

Silence stretched out a beat too long. "Where are you?"

"I'm at Logan Maxwell's farm." She could practically hear Porter's eyebrows hitting his hairline. "It's not what you think." Though even as she said it, she had dim memories of hauling him down to her on the sofa. She really hoped that was a dream. "I was too drunk to drive and I called him for a ride last night. I was apparently too drunk to go home, so I slept here. He's already out in the fields, and I really need to get home."

The words came out in a rush, and she could only hope he didn't pick up on her desperation.

After another infinitely long pause, he said, "I'll be by to get you shortly."

CHAPTER 5

*L*ogan toed off his muddy boots at the door and went into the house in search of coffee. He'd downed a cup before heading out for morning chores, but it hadn't been high-octane enough to make up for the restless night from having Athena under his roof and not in his bed. His brain had been all too happy to keep him awake with alternate scenarios in which he hadn't clung to his status as a gentleman. Alternate scenarios that would've left them both extremely satisfied. But he wasn't an asshole who'd take advantage of an inebriated woman. And as much as he wanted to revisit things with Athena, he didn't have any interest in being her rebound guy.

The dogs bumped at his knees in their haste to race over and assume the position beside the treat bucket.

"Yeah, yeah. I got it. Morning treats." He lifted the lid and dug a couple of biscuits out. "Wait," he ordered.

They both sat, perfectly still but for the swishing of their synchronized tails, as he carefully balanced the biscuits on the bridges of their snouts. Peep's eyes went a little crazed, but she didn't break the hold until he said, "Okay."

The coffee pot hadn't been touched since he'd left it, so he could only assume Athena wasn't up yet. Maybe he'd just take his coffee upstairs and check to make sure she was still among the land of the living. With visions of a full country breakfast—made by his hands, not hers—scrolling through his head, he climbed the stairs. Bacon, fried eggs, toast... Biscuits would be better, but he wasn't sure he had that kind of time. Either way, she'd need something to help combat the hangover, and he'd learned in his college years that a big, greasy breakfast usually did the trick.

The door to the guest room hung ajar. He lifted a hand to knock on the doorframe, and realized the room was empty. So was the adjoining bathroom. Logan frowned, wondering if she'd gone exploring. But she wasn't anywhere in the house and her purse and shoes were gone. She'd apparently snuck out while he'd been in the fields.

Maybe she'd been embarrassed? Why else wouldn't she leave some kind of note or something? But how the hell had she left? Had she called somebody else for a pickup now that it was morning? He hadn't heard a vehicle, but then he'd had the tractor cranked up.

It should've relieved him. He wasn't responsible for taking time out of his work day to get her back to the inn or her car. But given her emotional state the night before and the likelihood of the mother of all hangovers, he couldn't just let it go. What if she *didn't* have a ride and had gotten a wild hair to walk back to town? She was just stubborn enough to do it.

He poured his coffee into a travel mug and climbed in the truck before he could think better of it. She wasn't trudging down the side of the road, which didn't make him feel a whole lot better. How much of last night did she remember? Did she think something had happened between them? Was *that* why she'd bolted? At least he could put that fear to rest. If he could find her.

The inn was the obvious first stop. Judging from the cars lining the drive, everybody had shown up for breakfast. This would be boatloads of fun. He let himself in, heading straight back to the kitchen.

"Logan! What a lovely surprise." Pru beamed at him from the griddle where at least two pounds of bacon sizzled and popped.

From his place at the long, kitchen table, Xander lifted his coffee mug in greeting. "Hey man, what brings you over this way?"

Logan needed to decide fast what he was going to say here. A quick scan of the room showed his quarry wasn't present. Which left the truth or some kind of bald-faced lie. He'd never been any good at prevarication. "Is Athena here?"

"What do you want, Logan?"

He turned to see her standing in the doorway. She'd showered and looked about two steps above warmed-over death. The smudge of shadows deepened the gray of her eyes and only served to highlight the pallor of her skin. Her chin held a defiant tilt, and her stance said all shields were up. But her arms told a different story. They were crossed over her middle in a self-protective gesture that belied her fierce stance. Without a word, he took a step closer, studying her eyes. It wasn't anger he saw there, but devastation. This wasn't about the boyfriend or the cheating. That had been all temper last night, more a wound to her pride than her heart. What had happened?

"I came to check on you."

"I'm fine." Her tone was as hard and implacable as steel. But she wasn't nearly as sure of herself as she wanted them to believe. Beneath all that bravado, she was shaking.

"I don't think you are or you wouldn't have snuck out this morning without a word." He ignored the gasps from the table and continued walking toward her. "Nothing happened. You passed out on the couch with the dogs, so I took you up to the guest room to sleep it off."

Her face went impossibly paler. "I know exactly where I woke up this morning," she snarled.

"Okay, forgive me for interrupting, but exactly why are you biting Logan's head off?" Kennedy asked. "Because, from where I'm sitting, it sounds like you drank too much, and he picked you up and took care of you."

He saw the momentary flash of pain before her temper ignited.

"Why didn't you tell me?" she demanded. "Why didn't *any* of you think to tell me?"

Okay seriously, what the hell was going on?

"Tell you what?" Logan asked.

But she wasn't looking at him. Her glare seemed to be divided between her sisters and Xander, who looked as baffled as Logan felt.

Xander winced as realization struck. "Aw shit. I didn't even think."

For the love of... "Somebody want to tell me what's going on?"

Pru rescued the bacon and switched off the griddle. "Your farm is where Athena grew up."

Given everybody's chastened expressions and Athena's palpable fury, this was a big thing. Obviously the news had blindsided her, but for the life of him, he didn't understand why it was a big deal. A surprise, sure. One of those random, small-town coincidences. But not a reason for the raw emotional wound he saw on her face.

"I'm taking a walk." Without another word, she stalked out the back door and slammed it.

Pru jumped into the ensuing silence. "I'm sorry about that. She's—"

Logan just held up a hand. "Stop apologizing. If she wants to tell me, she'll do it herself." Without waiting for further commentary or questions, he followed her out.

She didn't have that much of a lead on him. Following her down the trail to Opal Springs was a helluva lot easier in the daylight than it had been last summer. A few times she paused to toss fulminating glares over her shoulder. Everything about her shouted at him to go the hell away. But he wasn't ready to leave her just yet. He had a feeling people were too inclined to leave her alone when she had these outbursts because they didn't see the pain underneath the anger.

At the springs, she climbed up on one of the flat rocks, fisting her hands and staring at the water as if she was contemplating jumping in. He just took a seat and waited in silence. He was a farmer. He knew patience.

"Why are you here, Logan?"

"Because you're upset, and it's something to

do with me. Maybe if you tell me, I can do something to fix it."

Bitter laughter scraped over his skin like sandpaper. "Got a time machine?"

He wondered if she wished she could go back in time to stop herself from getting involved with the douche who cheated on her.

"Can you go back and stop my mom from leaving or my dad from the drug overdose that institutionalized him when I was twelve?"

Whatever he'd expected, it wasn't that. As the question was rhetorical, he waited to see if she'd elaborate or tell him to go to hell.

She heaved a heart-heavy sigh.

"My parents were high school sweethearts. Got married right after graduation. Dad's grandparents were getting on in years, so they retired and gave my parents the farm as a wedding present. My mom wasn't what you could call excited about this development. She wanted bigger things than Eden's Ridge. But it was a roof over their heads and a living. Daddy wanted so much to be a farmer. He had this whole deal about wanting to be connected to the land. But he was just…bad at it. I think it was okay for the first few years. But farming is hard, risky work." She shot him a glance. "I don't have to tell you that."

He shook his head.

"I came along about the time the new wore off on their marriage. Then came the drought. It burned everything to a crisp and cracked the land. The next year was incessant rains that drowned and rotted the crops. And on and on it went. Every year was a new disaster. Every year they went deeper into debt."

That was pretty much Logan's worst nightmare. The idea that everything he'd built would be yanked away by the vagaries of Mother Nature.

"Eventually, when I was about eight, my mother gave him an ultimatum. Sell the farm and go get a more stable job or she was leaving. He wasn't willing to give up what he saw as his family legacy. So she left. And it was…well, it was what it was." She jerked her shoulders, shrugging off her mother's defection as just another one of those things. "I was Daddy's girl and he worked his ass off to make sure I didn't feel the loss too much. I took on too much responsibility too soon, but we got by. Just the two of us."

She went quiet, her throat working, the muscles of her face tightening as she fought not to cry.

"He had some good years. And then he had some more bad. He had to let some of the farm hands go, do more of it himself. What I didn't know at the time was he'd started using amphetamines to get through all that extra work. Just to keep him going because he couldn't bear to let go of the land that was slowly killing him. I got pulled out of class and talked to by the school counselor. She was concerned about the fact that I was falling asleep in class. Missing school. She wanted me to talk to somebody about the stress. So I did. And the next thing I know, a social worker's telling me to pack a bag and taking me away from my dad."

"That's how you ended up with Joan."

"Yeah. It was supposed to be temporary. But Daddy...he ended up in the hospital from an overdose. Whatever he took that last time wasn't pure. It was mixed with...God knows what. The doctors never did. Whatever it was essentially destroyed his brain. I was left without a father, the bank took the farm, and I never got to go home."

Until he'd taken her there.

Every instinct he had urged him to cross over and take her into his arms. But he didn't move. He understood her well enough to know she wouldn't want to be touched. But God, he ached for the little girl she'd been. He didn't know how to feel about her confession. There were too many layers to process just yet. He just knew he wanted to help, wanted to banish those shadows from her eyes and make her feel...better. Which was precisely the reason he'd gone into psychology in the first place.

And that turned out so well.

She finally turned to face him, her expression dialed somewhere between surprise and confusion. "I don't know why I just told you all that."

No way in hell was he admitting he'd gone to grad school to be a therapist. Athena Reynolds was the type who wouldn't trust shrinks. Why should she? They'd helped take her away. "I get that a lot." He hesitated. "That was your room with the stars."

She gave a jerky nod. "I'm sorry I flipped my shit." On a heavy sigh, she folded down to the rock beneath her, as if she simply couldn't stand anymore beneath the weight of what she carried. "Thanks for coming to my rescue last night."

Deflection. She didn't want to talk about her past anymore, and he couldn't blame her. He suspected that was more than she'd said about it to anyone, except probably her sisters, since it had happened.

"Anytime."

"What exactly did I say to you? Because it's all kinda fuzzy."

"It was pretty rambling, but the gist I got was that your boyfriend cheated on you with your sous chef and somehow that imploded your career."

She closed her eyes. Obviously that was another sore point. "Please don't say anything to my family. I haven't told them yet."

He lifted a hand. "I'm sorry, I have to document this momentous occasion. You actually said please."

The corner of her mouth twitched.

He sobered. "Of course, I'll keep it to myself. Are you okay? Or as okay as you can be right now?"

"Yeah."

She wanted solitude, and he wasn't the one to deny her.

"All right then. Unless you need anything else, I need to be getting on back to the farm."

"Go. Work. Thanks for listening."

"I've got two good ears and a shoulder if you ever need them."

She nodded and laid her head on her up-drawn knees.

He left her there, reluctantly climbing back up the ridge to his truck and work. But he couldn't help but wonder the whole way back about the fact that he was the one she'd confided in.

ATHENA HELD out for two days, recovering from the mutant hangover and the simple, earth-shattering shock of finding out Logan now owned her family's farm. She'd pulled out impressive avoidance tactics, even for her, to keep from discussing anything about him, the farm, or the mess in Chicago with her sisters. But by the time Maggie's name flashed across her phone—again—she understood her time was up. The options were to talk to Maggie or become the object of a family intervention.

She answered the phone. "I don't want to talk about it."

"Color me surprised. Pru told me about the farm. How are you feeling about all that?"

Her shoulders hunched up around her ears. "You know I hate the F word."

"Don't make me come out there."

She would, if she thought it necessary. But Maggie had already flown back to Tennessee so many times the past year—in the aftermath of Mom's death, all the insanity around custody of Ari, Kennedy and Xander's wedding, Ari's adoption, the holidays, and Pru and Flynn's wedding. Athena knew she'd be in hot water with her boss if she took more leave anytime soon.

She blew out a breath. "I'm...I don't know what I am."

"The word you're probably looking for is 'upset'. That thing you like to pretend you never are."

"Okay, fine. I'm upset. It really threw me for a loop." Understatement of the year. But she wasn't about to admit she'd been shaken to her very foundation by something so simple as waking up in her childhood bedroom.

"What's bothering you the most about this? You had to know it would've been sold to someone, the land worked by *someone*."

"Of course I knew that. On some level, anyway. But knowing and seeing are two different things." All that effort she'd spent not to see, not to look, undone.

"Is it that it's different than you remember? Home but not really?"

That trod far too close to the psychobabble she'd been avoiding since she went into the foster system. Her hands automatically fisted. "I don't know."

Maggie ignored the snappish tone. "Maybe you should go out there again to see it without hangover goggles. Nobody's their best when the entire percussion section of an orchestra is pounding away in their skull."

"Maybe." Maybe she really did need to face the past in a way she'd never had the chance to do. But facing the past meant facing Logan after she'd spilled her guts about all that emotional…crap. Was she ready for that?

"What was that about, anyway? You haven't been that drunk since right after Mom died."

She hadn't been that drunk even then.

The temptation to tell Maggie everything about Jayson and losing Olympus and the damned video—well on its way to a million views by now—was almost overwhelming. Her sister was a champion problem solver. Hell, it was what she did for a living out there in California. She'd have some kind of action plan put together inside a week.

But Athena simply wasn't ready.

"I'm going through some stuff."

"You know I'm here for you. For anything. Always."

"I know." And she did know, deep down in her soul. They'd been through hell together as kids. She could count on Maggie for anything. "I'll get around to telling you. I'm just not there yet."

Her sister drew in a slow, audible breath and

let it back out. "Okay. But no more trying to solve problems with vast quantities of alcohol."

"Promise. The temporary payoff was not worth the consequences."

"Whatever this is, take care of yourself, Sis."

"I will. I love you."

"Love you back. Talk soon."

Before she could lose her nerve, Athena grabbed her purse and headed downstairs. Flynn was in the office, updating information on the latest bookings. He looked up when she stuck her head in.

"Are you feeling better, then?"

She didn't think she'd ever quite get used to hearing her brother-in-law's smooth Irish brogue in East Tennessee. "Back among the land of the living. I thought I'd pick Ari up from her riding lesson this afternoon." It was the perfect excuse to head out to the farm.

One dark brow winged up. "Wanting to have a chat with Logan?"

She narrowed her eyes at him. "I just thought I'd save you the drive."

His lips quirked as he tried and failed to suppress a smile. "So that's the way of it. All right, then. I'd appreciate the help. I've some paperwork to catch up on around here."

With every mile closer to the farm, Athena's stomach curdled just a little bit more. What was she even supposed to *say* to Logan? She still couldn't quite believe she'd told him everything. But she was so used to people here *knowing.* What had happened to her father had been a topic of conversation for everybody in town when she was a child, and memories in Eden's Ridge ran long. Everyone had looked at her with pity or judgment after that, just waiting for her to follow in her father's footsteps and get into drugs because the apple didn't fall far from the tree, after all.

Her teen years had been marked by total desperation to escape the pitying looks and be something other than "that poor Bryson girl." Her drive for success had been as much about wanting to give them something else to talk about as it was the food. And it had worked.

People liked being able to say they knew a rising star. Somebody who was sort of famous. Somebody who'd made the Ridge proud.

Now all that was gone and she'd be "that poor Reynolds girl." New last name. Same backstabbing gossip.

And dammit, she'd told Logan everything. A huge part of her attraction to him had been that he wasn't from the Ridge and *didn't* know any of her past. Now he knew and he'd look at her differently. With pity or judgment or whatever the hell, just like everybody else. And that was her own damned fault.

It shouldn't matter. He'd been a wedding fling. A helluva one at that. But she genuinely *liked* him. Enough that they'd actually talked when she'd gone back to Chicago. That had kind of fallen away when she'd started dating Jayson. She realized now that she'd missed those conversations. Missed him. They'd been...almost friends. Now he'd be just another one of the things she'd lost.

On that dismal thought, she rolled to a stop

in front of the brightly-painted barn. Hating the feeling of vulnerability, she put on her favorite I-don't-give-a-shit armor and walked around the barn to the corral, where her niece was circling on a chestnut horse, her smile brighter than the afternoon sun. Athena softened, just a little. Ari's enthusiasm made hanging on to her bitch persona a challenge.

"Athena! Look! Look what I can do!" She nudged the horse into a trot and began to post.

Athena kept her eyes on the girl as she crossed over to lean on the paddock fence beside Logan. "Looking good, kid."

"She's been a quick study."

Under the weight of his gaze, she braced herself to look at him. But it wasn't the expected pity she saw. Surprised pleasure lit his hazel eyes, along with an undeniable flash of interest as he took her in from head to toe.

"I've never seen you in jeans before."

She hadn't given a thought to her outfit before coming out here. The ancient jeans and green t-shirt in ultra soft cotton were nothing to write home about. Comfortable. But he was looking at her exactly as he had the satin and lace she'd worn beneath her bridesmaid dress. Heat crawled up the back of her neck and into her cheeks as her brain flashed back to that night at Opal Springs.

She shrugged. "I guess you've mostly seen me at holidays and special occasions."

"Jeans suit you."

He did pretty amazing things for a pair of jeans himself. Not that she was going to go ogling his butt again with Ari mere yards away. And why was she even thinking about this right now? She'd broken up with Jayson not even two weeks ago. But standing here now, able to *feel* Logan's eyes on her like a caress, it was hard not to be all *Jayson who?*

"How's the head?" he asked.

"Better."

"Good."

She tensed, waiting for him to ask about the rest. Instead he shouted instructions to Ari. They watched her ride for another few minutes, standing in companionable silence. He didn't pry, and some of her tension unraveled. That was why she'd told him, she realized. Because he never forced anything. He let her tell him what she wanted to tell him, on her terms. She wondered if that was deliberate or just the way he was.

Her skin prickled with awareness of his proximity. She could've tipped her head to his shoulder or leaned to brush her arm against his. She didn't know what to do with that desire, though certainly it was better than the self-pity she'd been wallowing in on the drive out.

She'd never intended things with him to go further than a one-time thing. An indulgence. She'd seen him and she'd wanted. That should've been it. An enjoyable scratching of an itch. But then he'd been more. Turned out, the thoughtful, scruffy-faced farmer totally worked for her. His calm, unruffled demeanor was unarguably appealing. He never let her emotional storms—and he'd been witness to a few of them by now—bother him in the least.

That was...oddly refreshing. She could admit to herself now that if they'd been in the same place after the wedding, she'd have pursued him.

We're in the same place now.

She very nearly lifted a hand to brush that devil right off her shoulder. As gratifying as another fling with him would be, she didn't need the distraction. There was major life shit to figure out.

Still, it was hard not to engage in a little *what if.* Her mind conjured up an image of him carrying her through the house as she nibbled along his throat, his jaw, and made his muscles coil tight. He laid her down on the sofa, and she pulled that big, work-hardened body down over her to take what she wanted—

"Okay, I think we're done for the day," he called. "Cool him down, groom him, and put away your tack."

Ari saluted. "On it."

Athena gripped the rail hard enough her knuckles turned white. She'd asked him what she'd said to him. She hadn't asked what she'd *done*.

He frowned at her. "You okay?"

"Fine." She forced her lips to curve. Knowing her niece's penchant for eavesdropping, she asked, "Do you have time to give me a little tour?"

"Sure."

As Ari began to walk her mount in slower circles, Logan led Athena to a two-seater ATV. At the sound of the engine, the dogs burst free of a field and made a beeline toward them, dancing around the vehicle with happy barks before racing off ahead. They made her smile, reminding her of Samwise, the mutt she'd had growing up. He'd been some combination of hound, shepherd, and collie, made for running, and she'd adored him. He was buried in the apple orchard, beneath his favorite tree.

Logan drove her from one end of the farm to the other, pointing out crops, talking about plans. It was beautiful. Lush with rich earth and new, spring growth. He'd expanded beyond the basic crops and kitchen garden they'd had to include livestock. A small herd of cattle, goats, sheep. She'd seen chickens back by the barn. And, of course, the horses. He'd also added a series of hoop houses to extend the growing season and provide assorted produce year-round for the community supported agriculture program he'd started. He told her about his intention to build a bigger four-season greenhouse to replace the small one he'd experimented with over the winter. He was full of plans and dreams and ways to expand. Listening to him talk, Athena could see it —both what he'd done, what he wanted to do. There was something somehow soothing about seeing the land's potential unlocked and fully realized. It helped ease some ache to know that it hadn't gone to waste, hadn't been ruined.

At the top of a hill on the far side of the property, he parked. "This is my favorite spot. From here I can see almost the whole farm. The house. The barn. The outbuildings."

It spread out below them, a picture of pastoral beauty.

"Your spread is bigger than what we had," she observed.

"The guy before me bought up a fair chunk of the surrounding acreage to add to the original farm. I bought up more. I wanted the room for crop diversification."

"I still can't get over what you've done here. What you've made of this place. This was my father's greatest dream. Not one he ever came anywhere close to achieving. He struggled so much."

"I still struggle. As you said, farming is tough. In a lot of ways it's like playing futures on the stock market. You can do all the right things and Mother Nature can still decide you're not worthy and destroy everything. I've been lucky on that front, so far. My issue's been a lot more with exposure and making a profit competing against big agriculture."

This, at least, was something she knew about. "You should make contacts with the

restaurant scene in Nashville and the surrounding areas. Olympus has contracts with
farmers all over Illinois to get the best of the
best."

"I've made some, but a lot of them are put
off by the cost of organic produce. Particularly
produce that has to come from four hours
away, when there are other farms closer.
They've all gotta deal with the current economy
like everybody else. And then there's the trans-
portation costs and all the rest. I'm doing okay,
but I'd like to expand more."

She knew what it took to work a farm. She
couldn't begin to imagine how much he'd sunk
into this place, both in money and blood, sweat,
and tears, to make it thrive. She wondered how
he'd come to be here, doing this. It wasn't
something she'd asked him in their conversations all those months ago, and she didn't feel
quite like asking him now. She had other things
on her mind.

"Logan, I need to ask you something."

He folded his arms loosely over the steering wheel and shifted to look at her. "Shoot."

How to put this? "Do I have something to apologize for from the other night?"

"You don't need to apologize for asking for a ride. I'd way rather you call than try to drive. That was the smart thing to do."

"No, I mean—" She huffed a breath and took the bull by the horns. "Did I try to jump you?"

He pursed his lips, clearly considering his answer.

Shit.

"You might have made it clear that you were interested in a repeat performance of last summer."

Not much embarrassed her. She was un-apologetically herself pretty much all the time. But this... Covering her burning face with her hands, she wished she could sink into the ground beneath them. "I'm sorry."

"I'm not."

Spreading her fingers, she peered through

them to see his face. "You're not sorry I tried to maul you?"

"I'm not sorry you're still interested on some level. So am I. If you'd been anywhere approaching sober, you'd have woken up in a very different bed. But you weren't, so I stopped." He shrugged. "I don't see that as something to apologize for. If you decide you want to go there without the alcohol, I'm ready, willing, and able."

Direct and to the point. She appreciated that in a person. So she opted to respond in kind. "My life is a fucking mess right now, Logan."

"Because the asshole broke your heart or because of the imploded career thing?"

"My heart is broken because of the career thing. But I wasn't in love with the asshole."

"Does it make me a jackass if I say good?"

Her lips quirked. "It makes you honest. I find I appreciate that even more now than I did before."

"Then in the name of honesty, let me just say that I want to be here for you. Whether that's just as a friend or as a naked distraction."

A shudder ran through her body as she imagined his hands on her skin, stroking, stoking the heat inside her. "You have no idea how appealing an offer that is."

"An irresistible one, I hope." The flash of his grin against that close-cropped beard had lust unspooling in her belly.

"I'm probably going to kick myself for this later, but I think, for now, for your sake, I need to avoid the naked. You deserve better than being a rebound guy."

"While a part of me is inclined to say that rebound sex is better than no sex, the smarter part agrees with you. So no naked. For now. But the friend thing is still on the table."

She sighed. "I could really use a friend."

"Then consider me yours."

His gaze caught hers and held. Tension snapped between them, and for a moment, she thought he'd blow the whole friend declaration all to hell and kiss her. She wanted him to.

Instead, he pulled back on a rueful smile. "This may be harder than I thought."

"More trouble than it's worth to try?"

"Hell no. You're worth the effort."

As he put the ATV into gear, she decided so was he.

CHAPTER 6

Spring planting was finally finished.
Thank Christ.

Filthy, tired, and starving, Logan came in
from the fields, thrilled to be done before dark.
He'd earned a beer. And a shower. Maybe a beer
in the shower. Yeah. That'd be a fitting reward
for his accomplishment. Maybe he'd haul his
ass into town to the tavern for a meal he didn't
have to wrangle himself. He checked his watch.
It was early yet. Maybe he could convince
Athena to join him.

He hadn't seen her since she'd stopped by

the farm a few days ago, but they'd been texting and had had a few more of those late-night conversations they'd managed in the wake of the wedding. Well, late for him. His farmer's hours and her chef's hours didn't have a ton of overlap. She still hadn't shared any details about the whole exploding career thing. He'd considered hitting up Google to see if it was a newsworthy kind of explosion. But if it was, he didn't want to be one more yahoo invading her privacy. And he could admit to himself, he wanted her to tell him herself, in her own time. He wanted to earn that kind of trust. So he'd be patient.

Head full of her, Logan stored his equipment in the pole barn and headed for the house. He drew up short at the sight of Porter's truck in the drive. Changing direction, he circled around to the far side of the big red barn—when would he start thinking of it as the stable? Porter leaned on the rail of the little corral, talking to Sebastian. Inside the fence was a pair of the sorriest-looking specimens of horse

Logan had ever seen. Each rib stood out in stark relief along their sides and their heads hung low, nary an ear or tail twitch between them.

"Damn. They're even worse than you described." Logan joined Porter at the rail.

Sebastian's jaw tensed. "I'd like a few hours alone with the asshole who let them get to this state."

"Are we gonna have problems with him?" Up to this point, the rescues they'd gotten had been willingly surrendered. Animals whose owners could no longer afford their upkeep. These were the result of a judicial mandate.

"Law's on our side. He lost the case and them. If that's not enough to keep him away, I've got no problem sending a clearer message." The dark glint in Sebastian's eyes suggested he'd enjoy it.

"Guess we'll see."

"The vet's been by," Sebastian continued. "They're extremely malnourished, obviously. Both have thrush in their feet and their hooves are overgrown. The bay there has a wound on her shoulder—probably from a barbed wire fence. That's infected. Beyond all that, their spirits are broken. This is a level of profound neglect I can barely wrap my head around."

"Think they're gonna make it?" Porter asked.

"Could go either way. They'll be treated for their medical issues. With some proper nutrition and TLC, their physical condition should improve. After that, it'll be up to them. They have to choose life."

If anyone could coax these horses to make that choice, it was Sebastian. The former Army Ranger had been through a similar struggle after his separation from the military. He'd made the choice for life himself and come here. Sometimes he had to renew that choice, but over the months he'd been here, working with the horses, Logan had seen that choice become easier. With them he had a reason to keep making it.

"You'll convince them it's worthwhile," he said.

Sebastian just grunted.

"If the horses are settled for a bit, I brought beer and pizza," Porter announced. "Figured y'all could help me eat it."

"Yeah?" Logan perked up at the idea he wouldn't have to drive to town for sustenance. "I can get behind that."

Sebastian shook his head. "Not me. The farrier's making a special trip out this evening to take care of those hooves so we can get a jump on treating the thrush. And I want to see if they'll let me close enough to wash and groom them. They're skittish yet."

"Another time then."

"I'm gonna head on up to shower off my day. Come on inside when you're ready and make yourself at home."

Logan detoured through the kitchen and snagged that beer. He drank half as he stripped down, switched on the water to scalding. Once steam billowed through the bathroom, he stepped into the shower, tucking the bottle into the caddy beside the body wash. The steady spray beat at his sore muscles, sluicing over his head and shoulders to rinse away the grime. Because it just felt damned good, he lingered, sipping at the other half of his beer as his body relaxed.

He was a man who appreciated simple pleasures. A cold beer, hot shower, good food, and the company of a friend. About the only thing that would've made his mood even better would've been a gray-eyed, sharp-tongued beauty joining him in the shower. The image of Athena in nothing but skin, hair slicked back like a seal as she swam through Opal Springs with about as much agility was burned into his brain. It was easy enough to picture her here, in his shower. That, too, was simple.

Someday. Maybe.

By the time he made it downstairs, he felt considerably more human. The sound of voices and the scent of herbs and pepperoni drew him into the kitchen, where he found Xander kicked back against the counter, a beer in his hand.

"We having a party?"

"I am blessedly off-duty. Thank Christ." Xander lifted the beer in toast.

"You're off-duty and not spending the night with your wife?"

"Kennedy has to work tonight. I figured I'd come out, have a look at those horses in their new home, and steal a beer. Besides, game's on."

Indeed, one of them had switched on the TV. The faint murmur of an announcer's voice from the living room underscored the conversation. Maybe this really was just a simple case of drop in and hang out. But Logan suspected there was more at play here than an impromptu social call.

He ducked into the fridge, grabbed another beer. "We're second string. We get it."

"We'll take the dregs," Porter agreed.

"So the good Sheriff here came out to check on the horses. What about you? Why the pizza delivery out here in the sticks?" Logan asked.

"I wanted to check on Sebastian." It wasn't

the first time and wouldn't be the last when Porter followed up on his old Army buddy.

"He hasn't needed checking on in a while," Logan pointed out.

"Old habits, man." A wealth of loyalty earned in battle underlaid those three words.

He knew that was at least half the reason Porter had suggested Sebastian for the job. "I'm not seeing any signs you should worry about. He's still got some insomnia, but the horses, the work, have been good for him. The lessons and interactions with people will be good for him, too, when we get to them."

"Good."

They loaded up plates with the pizza Porter had shoved in the oven to keep warm and moved into the living room to watch the game. Lured by the prospect of scraps, Bo and Peep appeared at the door from wherever they'd spent their afternoon. As soon as Xander let them inside, they made a beeline to the living room, camping out at attention, just waiting for somebody to toss them a crust.

"They act like you don't even feed them," Porter observed.

"Spoiled rotten, the both of them." Which was entirely true, but Logan wouldn't have it any other way.

Xander propped his feet on the scarred coffeetable and tipped back his beer.

Recognizing the tell, Logan braced himself.

"So, what's going on between you and Athena?"

Not nearly enough. But he couldn't say that. Instead, Logan took a pull on his own beer. "What are you talking about?"

"Don't pull that evasive shit with me. I'm a cop, not an idiot. I could tell the other morning that there's...something between you. Why the hell did she even call you to pick her up? I didn't think you even knew each other beyond family functions."

"We're friends." Okay, maybe that was a stretch, but they were working on it.

Porter snorted. "Is that what they're calling it now?"

Irritated at being cornered in his own damned living room, Logan wondered if Pru had been talking. "What's that supposed to mean?"

"Just that you two have never given off friend vibes. I wondered if something happened between you two at the wedding last summer."

"No way," Xander insisted.

Caught off-guard by Porter's observation, Logan didn't quite manage to don his poker face.

Porter pointed. "See?"

Xander's mouth dropped open. "Seriously?"

On a sigh, Logan accepted that the cat was out of the bag. "Okay yes. We hooked up at your wedding."

"Called it." On a satisfied smirk, Porter split a crust in two and tossed it to the dogs, who snapped the pieces out of the air before turning their attention to Xander and the slice he held limp in his hand.

"I didn't. Dude."

"Why are you so surprised? She's sexy, smart, and the things that woman can do in a kitchen...Jesus, I've had dreams about what she can do with bacon."

"Please let that not be a euphemism. That's my sister-in-law."

Logan rolled his eyes. "So?"

"It's not like you to sniff around somebody else's territory."

"I'm not. She dumped the douchebag."

Remembering the pizza in his hand, Xander nodded and bit in. "I wondered. She hasn't said anything to Kennedy. Pru either, far as I can tell."

"Maggie's worried about her," Porter added.

"Because of her whole reaction to the farm or something else?" Logan asked.

"There's that. But in general. I was pretty worried myself when I picked her up here the other morning."

"I wondered how the hell she got back to the inn."

"I haven't seen her that rattled in...hell, I'm

not sure I've ever seen her that rattled except when she realized her daddy was never coming home and staying with Joan wasn't gonna be temporary."

"He's still living?"

"Yeah. If you can call the state he's in living," Xander said.

Logan turned his attention back to Porter. "You were there then?"

It was easy to forget Porter had been one of the Reynolds sisters' many foster siblings.

"Yeah. I'd been in and out for a couple years at that point. I saw all kinds of reactions to kids fresh in the system. Most of us came from shitty homes. She didn't. And being yanked out like she was...she never got over that."

"Why was she taken from him?" Logan remembered she said she'd been pulled out of class by a counselor about falling asleep in school.

"He had a drug problem," Xander explained. "Somebody saw him with a guy who was a known dealer and put a bug in the ear of the right person. They had Athena questioned by the school counselor and a social worker. It was enough for the state to temporarily take custody while they investigated. Then he overdosed."

"She trusted the wrong people and they took away her control," Logan mused. And she'd spent all these years trying to get it back.

"Be careful," Xander warned.

"Is that for me or for her?"

"You. She's got a hard shell."

Logan felt a prick of irritation on Athena's behalf. How many people saw only that? "You'd be wrong about that. That whole thing is a defense mechanism."

"Dude, above all, do *not* psychoanalyze her. You will lose your balls. She absolutely hates that shit."

"That's like telling me not to see the grass is green."

"You know what I mean. I'm just saying she's anti-therapists."

Logan lifted his last slice of pizza. "Then it's a good thing I'm a farmer."

COWARDICE TASTED of stone ground cornbread. It crumbled, soaked in sweet cream butter, into Athena's mouth, and it didn't even matter that she'd burned her tongue. This wasn't about pleasing anyone but herself. That was what the past two-and-a-half weeks had been about, after all.

Two-and-a-half weeks since the disaster. Two-and-a-half weeks she'd been licking her wounds and hiding the truth. Two-and-a-half weeks she'd been waiting for the other shoe to drop in the form of one of her sisters finding out about Olympus. Because she really didn't want to be the one to tell them. She didn't want to admit what she'd done. How she'd screwed up.

It was only a matter of time. It surprised her none of them had figured it out already. But

Maggie was busy as hell running someone's world. Pru was all focused on the baby and Ari and the spa expansion, not to mention her sexy new husband. Kennedy was likewise occupied by newlywed bliss and all the promo for her upcoming book. Their distraction had bought Athena a reprieve. But that wouldn't last.

She'd been hoping to have her next steps in place before she admitted it, so she could control the spin and make it look like a move she'd made on purpose. But that would necessitate actually putting out feelers in the foodie community, and she hadn't done that either. All she'd done was hide out, taking over the inn's kitchen, pitching in with whatever other chores she, Flynn, and Ari could manage to wrest from Pru. Because she was afraid of the answer. Afraid if she reached out, she'd get nothing but crickets—or worse, derision, in return. Deep down, she was afraid that all her value was tied up in Olympus and without it, she was nothing but a farm girl from Tennessee who happened to know a lot about cooking.

Miserable, she forked another bite into her mouth.

Her phone rang. She didn't want to admit she'd begun keeping it on her so she wouldn't miss texts from Logan. But he'd been the one sort-of bright spot these past weeks. A balm to her wounded ego.

Master of Carbs flashed across the screen. Moses. Relief and longing washed over her in equal measure. Friend and colleague, Moses pulled no punches. He'd talk her through this and bully or browbeat her into action.

"Please tell me you're calling to give me the shot in the ass I need to get over this shit."

"Athena, I am so sorry." The rumble of his voice rolled over the line, sparking new worries in its wake. He wouldn't be apologizing now for what had happened with the video, so what was he talking about?

"For what?"

In the beat of silence, she could almost see him closing those dark eyes and rubbing a broad-palmed hand over the head he kept shaved. "Shit."

"Moses. Tell me."

"Don't shoot the messenger."

"I've lost my restaurant and become a viral video. I don't know how much worse it can get."

He blew out a breath. "Olympus lost its Michelin star."

She wanted to ask him to repeat himself, but couldn't form the words. His statement echoed through her skull like a gong, resonating through every pore and crack, until she thought one more blow would shatter her completely.

"Tell me," she whispered.

Forty-five minutes later, she was still sitting at the kitchen table, phone clutched in her hand, though Moses had said goodbye already. The sound of voices and footsteps from the foyer didn't manage to get her moving. No more hiding. She wasn't that good an actress or liar.

Kennedy came in with Ari, the two of them

laughing over something. The laughter died away as soon as they caught sight of her.

"Athena?" Kennedy straddled the long bench beside her, laying a hand on her arm. "What happened? What's wrong?"

Athena didn't look at her. She swallowed against a throat gone dry. "Get Pru."

Kennedy looked to Ari, who bolted from the room as if lives depended on it. And maybe Athena's did, in a sense.

They came back a couple minutes later.

"Athena? Honey? What is it?" Pru slid onto the bench on the other side. "Is it your dad?"

She shook her head, still not looking at her sisters. "Call Maggie." She couldn't endure going through this more than once.

Kennedy dialed from her own phone, setting it on speaker.

"Kennedy, I don't have but a minute. There's a—"

"It's me," Athena croaked.

Maggie sucked in a breath. "Hang on." In the background, she could hear her sister giving orders to her assistant to hold all calls and let somebody know she'd be unavoidably late to the meeting. A door shut. Then Maggie was back on the line. "Okay. You have my undivided attention. What's going on?"

Because her lips trembled, Athena pressed them together until she thought she could speak without crying. "I lied. I'm not home because Olympus is being renovated." And she told them everything, editing out some of the gory details of what she'd walked in on for Ari's sake.

The omissions didn't stop her niece from snarling, "That bastard!"

It was almost enough to wrangle a smile.

"Ari," Pru warned.

"Well, he is!"

"She is not wrong. I don't know if the two of them planned this. Probably not. But the end result is the same. I'm out. Olympus isn't mine anymore."

"Oh, honey, I'm so, so sorry." Kennedy

wrapped an arm around her shoulders and squeezed.

"It gets worse. There's a video of our confrontation in the kitchen. It's gone viral."

Of course, that led to a trip to YouTube. They all watched in silence as her reckless behavior unfolded in all its glory. When it was done, nobody seemed to know what to say. This wasn't the first tantrum she'd had. Wouldn't be the last. But it was the only one that would have lasting impact.

"You always did have a hell of an arm," Kennedy observed. "Though you were better with a softball."

Athena snorted, but the sound came out somewhere between a laugh and a sob. "It gets worse."

"There's *more?*" Pru asked. Her arm slid around Athena's waist, as if she sensed this was the worst part.

"Olympus lost its Michelin star."

"Under somebody else's leadership," Ari put in.

Athena shook her head, wishing it were that simple. "That's not how it works. They wouldn't yank it over one bad meal. It would be a product of several visits over time, which means that loss is on me. *I* lost my Michelin star. I failed to keep up the standards. And I've torpedoed my career but good. No one's gonna want to touch me after all this."

They surrounded her in hugs, talking over each other trying to comfort. Much as she'd resisted opening up, this was why she'd come home. This unqualified defense and support.

"We'll figure this out, as a family," Pru insisted.

"I'm not sure what help y'all can be helping me find another job," Athena said.

"Duh," Ari said. "You should work here."

"Excuse me?"

"She's got a point." Kennedy leaned back against the table. "The fact is, though we're called The Misfit Inn, we're actually more of a B and B since we only do breakfast. True inns offer full-service meals. We could make that switch. Amp things up again."

Stay and join the family business. It was the immediate and obvious answer. But it wasn't what Athena wanted or needed to hear at the moment.

"I can't make a decision like that right now." She'd spent so much time and effort to escape this place. How could she even consider moving back for good? Wasn't that giving up? Settling?

"You don't have to make a decision right now," Maggie pointed out. "Take some time. You said you're covered financially through the end of the year. Maybe you want to do some experimenting in the kitchen. You'll have options. They just may not be exactly what you originally thought."

Yeah. That's what she was afraid of.

CHAPTER 7

Are you still up for that distraction? Logan stared at Athena's text for ten full seconds before responding. Was she serious? She'd been pretty firm when she'd said no to that last week, so what had changed her mind?

"Only one way to find out."

He thumbed back a reply. **Any time.**

The message showed as read, but though he waited, there were no little dots showing her typing a response. Had he scared her off?

Bo and Peep bolted up, barking, just before

the knock sounded. A blur of black and white fur, they raced to the door. He waded through them and opened it to find Athena on the other side. Well, that explained the lack of a follow-up text.

"That was fast."

"I was at the end of the driveway." She bent, dropping her arms from where they'd been folded across her middle to give the dogs a rub. When she straightened, she had on what he thought of as her defiant mask. Shoulders back, chin lifted. It was a posture of confidence, yet it couldn't hide that her cheeks looked pale and the skin around her eyes was pinched.

Not waiting for an invitation, she stepped inside, lifting a hand to his chest and skimming it up around the back of his neck.

When she would've drawn his mouth to hers, Logan gripped her shoulders. "Slow down."

Temper flared in her eyes. But there was something else, too. "Slow wasn't exactly what I had in mind."

"What's wrong?"

"You're still talking."

"Something upset you."

She huffed out a breath. "What does that matter?"

"Call me old-fashioned, but when I take you to bed, I want your mind on me."

"That's the challenge and the point of being a distraction, Farmer Boy." She shot for a flirtatious grin and missed by a mile.

Logan searched her face, skimming a thumb across her cheek. "If I'm supposed to distract you, it'd help if I knew what I was distracting you from."

Her expression turned mulish, and he expected her to shove out of his grip and storm out. But her need, whatever it was, evidently outweighed her temper.

"I lost my star."

He frowned, not understanding. Was this some piece of jewelry with sentimental attachment?

At his lack of comprehension, she huffed. "My Michelin star for Olympus."

He didn't know much about them other than it was a big freaking deal. "They can take them back?"

"Yes, they can." She did pull away then, stalking past him toward the kitchen.

Logan trailed after her. "Is this what you meant when you said your career had imploded?"

"Oh, no, this is the icing on the shit sundae." Her words were punctuated by the slam of cabinet doors.

She didn't look at him, instead opening every cabinet and drawer, pulling things out from the fridge and pantry as she spilled out the whole, awful story. Logan said nothing. He had no idea what she was making, but he understood she needed to move, needed to cook in order to get through this. She was taking control in the only way she could.

"I was so fucking driven, Logan. I wanted to be successful in my field to prove something.

To myself. To everybody where I came from. I needed to prove that I could *be* somebody. I was so hungry for that, and it drove me through the ranks fast. There was shit about all that I didn't like, but the success…the success was worth enduring it. And once I had that—once I had my star and my James Beard award, I could've walked away. I did what I set out to do. I was something, some*one*, damn it." The thunk of the knife as she chopped an onion echoed like machine-gun fire through the room.

He wanted to tell her that she *was* someone. That she always had been. But she wouldn't believe it. This was how she'd defined herself for years.

"You got both those things, but you stayed in. Why?"

"Because of the money. Not that it's massive compared to other fields, but it meant I could better provide for my father. I could finally get him out of the state facility he'd been in for years, into somewhere better, nicer. I was going to buy out the controlling shares of Olympus after that. But long-term care facilities are expensive. So expensive. So my five-year plan turned into more like fifteen. And it started to wear on me."

He couldn't even begin to imagine having to carry that burden from so young an age. Did she have any idea how strong she was to have lasted as long as she had? Anyone else would have long ago crumbled under the weight of it.

Athena paused to pound out some chicken breasts between two pieces of waxed paper with a cast iron skillet. "The fact is, I've been skating the edge of serious burnout for more than a year. I was at the edge, then Mom died, and I just shut down."

"I'd think that's a major part of the grief process. You lost a parent. That's hard under the best of circumstances. And you weren't expecting it. That made it worse. It takes time to get over that."

"My field is competitive. There is no time for long recoveries. I was relying on my old recipes, unable to create anything new. Wondering if I was ever going to be able to do it again."

Losing control of the one area she'd built her life and career around would've cut her off at the knees.

"What do you call what you're doing right now?"

She glanced down at the chicken and vegetables and shrugged. "Therapy? Walking down memory lane? I don't know."

"You literally walked into my kitchen with zero idea of what I had to work with and have thrown together something that smells pretty fantastic in less time than other people would stare into the freezer wondering what's for dinner."

"It's easy to work with farm-fresh ingredients."

That she'd minimize her abilities irritated him. "This isn't because of ingredients, Athena. You're amazingly talented. And this is…I don't know…the epitome of the whole farm-to-table movement."

"Farm to table was just an economic reality for me growing up. We lived on what Dad could grow, so I was canning, drying, smoking, freezing, whatever from the time I was knee-high. It was practical, and I was fortunate enough to find it fun. But it's not haute cuisine, not what I was trained to do. This is just…compulsion."

It smelled a hell of a lot better than compulsion to him, and he didn't really understand the difference between haute cuisine and farm-to-table cooking. He'd eaten at farm-to-table restaurants before, had contracts with a few of them. It was pretty high-end stuff compared to the standard bar and grill. Did she draw a line between the two because anything that close to the farm reminded her of the life that was ripped away?

Before he could ask, she picked up the thread of her story. "Anyway, when I started struggling creatively, Mari—that's my back-stabbing sous chef—helped me fill in the gaps, and I skated by. Part of me wonders if she was setting me up, even then." She drizzled olive oil in the cast iron skillet. "Doesn't matter. It's over and done with now. And the truth of the matter is, no matter how much I hate how things went down, there's relief in finally being free of the suffocating weight of expectation and the life I've had in Chicago."

Athena braced her hands against the counter and, for the first time since she'd started, lifted her eyes to his. "I haven't been able to admit that. Because it's admitting that, in the end, I didn't actually want the dream I thought I wanted, the dream I worked so damned hard to achieve. And that feels like failure."

She'd admitted it to him. And maybe this was really why she'd come here tonight. Not because of the chemistry, not because she really needed distraction, but because she needed the catharsis of sharing this vulnerability with someone safe, someone who wouldn't judge her, someone who wasn't part of the history that had made her who she was.

Logan wanted to be that safe space for her. It was why he'd so readily agreed to friendship. He knew building that foundation first was what she needed. But he hadn't anticipated what earning her trust would mean to him. Other than seeing his farm come to fruition, nothing he'd worked for since he left grad school had felt as gratifying.

Recognizing her trust for the gift it was, he wanted to give her something back, to soothe this hurt however he could. "It's not failure if the dream changes. You think I always wanted to be a farmer?"

She laid the chicken breasts into the spitting, popping oil. "To be honest, I hadn't given it a lot of thought. Which makes me a self-centered bitch."

"No it doesn't. We haven't had that kind of relationship where we talk about much of the personal." But he hoped, with this conversation, that was changing.

"What did you want to be?"

"Well, there's what I wanted to be and what

my parents expected me to be. My dad is an attorney. My grandfather was a judge. I was expected to go into the law. Maybe politics."

Athena's brows arched. "You, a politician?"

"It'd be a miserable existence, that's for damned sure. I was pre-law. Double majored in psych and political science. And when it came time to apply to law school, I applied to grad school instead."

"In what?"

He hesitated, but there was no hiding the truth. "Psychology."

Her shoulders went stiff.

Logan pretended not to notice. "My parents were pissed. But they got over it. I'd have an advanced degree, after all. They had visions of me going on to get my PhD, being Dr. Logan Maxwell. For a little while, I bought into that, but by the time I got through the coursework and into my master's thesis, I knew that wasn't going to make me happy either. So I bailed the last year of my master's program and didn't graduate. Instead, I bought this place."

His answer seemed to mollify her. She flipped the chicken and added the vegetables she'd sautéed back to the pan before sliding the whole thing into the oven and setting a timer. "How did you afford it on a grad student's income?"

"I had a trust fund from my mother's parents. I poured every last cent of it into this place, which my parents considered just the latest in a long line of mistakes." He skirted around the island to join her by the stove. "You talk about wanting to prove yourself. I get that. We've all got something to prove. I've got to prove I can make this farm a success, to show my parents that bailing in the last year of grad school wasn't a mistake, that walking away from the life they wanted for me wasn't a mistake."

"Does it make you happy?" It wasn't a question he'd expected from her.

"Yeah. Every backbreaking minute of it."

"Then it wasn't a mistake." Her instant acceptance of his choice was balm to a wound he hadn't let himself think about.

He curved a hand around her waist and pulled her closer. "Did Olympus make you happy?"

"Not for a long time."

"Then no matter how things concluded, walking away was the right choice. You'll figure out the next step."

"I wish I felt more confident about that. I wish Mom were still alive. Nobody ever understood how to deal with me better than Joan." She laid a hand against his chest and frowned. "Although, you seem to be managing better than anybody else, just now. I don't quite know what to do with that."

"Enjoy it?" he suggested.

Her lips curved a little. "That was why I came over here, after all."

This time he met her halfway when she lifted to him. Instead of the temper and grief, he tasted something softer in her kiss. An unexpected vulnerability that made him want to give her tenderness instead of heat. She wasn't a woman used to softness, wasn't someone who sought it out. He understood she didn't trust it. But she needed it, whether she knew it or not.

So he took his sweet time, lingering over her lips, savoring the flavor of her as she opened to him, let him go deeper. Layer by layer, he coaxed his way past her defenses, until she wrapped around him, warm and pliant, the tension she'd brought lost beneath sensation. This was a different kind of release, one he hoped was more profound and lasting than the fast, mindless one she'd come for. It was another level of trust, one that rocked him to his core and made him realize that nothing with this woman could be simple or casual after this. Not for him. And he didn't want it to be.

At the sound of the oven timer, he eased back. "Do you need to get that?"

She reached out without looking and swatted at the panel until the buzzing shut up. The dazed look in her eyes made him want to grin.

"You're really good at that."

"You did ask for distraction."

"So I did." On a sigh, she stepped back from him, grabbing a potholder to remove the skillet from the oven. "You didn't ask for dinner."

He hadn't asked for any of this, and still he wanted. But not yet. He'd meant what he said about when he took her to his bed. She wasn't ready for that yet.

"No, but a smart man knows better than to turn it down. What are we having?"

"CODE DASH AND STASH!" Ari sailed into the kitchen with all the energy of one of Logan's border collies.

Athena glanced up from the notepad of recipe scraps she'd been working on for the past twenty minutes. "A code what?"

"Code Dash and Stash. We got a call that our couple from Oregon caught an earlier flight. They're going to be here within the hour."

"Don't we have a policy of no check-ins before three?"

"Yeah but we try to work with folks when we can. Dad went over to the spa to see if there's room to book them for some treatments or something to buy more time, but we need to check Redwood to see if we can't go ahead and get it turned. C'mon. We can divide and conquer."

Spurred by the girl's sense of urgency, Athena pushed to her feet and followed her upstairs to the designated guest room. "What are you even doing home this early?"

"Half day at school. I propose we finish up with this, then you teach me to make something amazing as a snack, and we watch some *Great British Bake Off.*"

"Sounds like you've mapped out the whole afternoon."

"Oh yeah, I've got plans. Cooking lessons. Some GBBO to soften you up, put you in a good mood. Then I'm totally going to quiz you about Logan."

Athena shot her niece the side eye. "Doesn't it defeat the purpose if you warn me you're going to quiz me about Logan?"

"Nah. I figure it gives you time to resign yourself."

Ari shoved open the door to Redwood. The bed had already been stripped, and the scent of lemon verbena indicated the bathroom had already been cleaned, so they just needed to reassemble.

"There's nothing to resign myself to. There's nothing going on with me and Logan."

Ari pivoted and pursed her lips, one brow arched. "Please."

Her absolute certainty had a snort of laughter bubbling up in Athena's chest. "You keep thinking that cupcake. I'm gonna get fresh linens."

The girl had a soft, gooshy, romantic heart. It was sweet, really. When you weren't the target of her interrogations. But Athena could hardly answer questions when she didn't know what was going on with him herself. Despite her intentions the other night, she hadn't slept with him. She'd expected a few hours of naked distraction, and she'd gotten conversation instead. But that kiss...

She clutched the stack of sheets to her chest as she remembered the feel of his mouth on hers. It hadn't been all the tongues and teeth and heat she'd expected. That she'd been prepared for. It was what she'd thought she wanted. His kiss had been slow and patient, as if he had all the time in the world to just savor the taste of her. It had been unexpected and oddly devastating, leaving her more off-balance than she'd ever been with him.

They'd ended up sharing the meal she'd compulsively made and talking for hours. She felt better for it. More settled than she had since this whole toxic mess began. This was more than the shallow flirtation they'd shared last summer. This was the beginnings of legitimate friendship. Even as she'd been trying to wrap her brain around that, he'd nudged her out the door toward home, somehow doing it without making her feel rejected, despite the lack of a follow-up kiss.

In the days since, she'd considered that, like his dogs, he was herding her where he wanted her, which was...where? Toward something more than friends or naked distraction. Athena didn't know how she felt about that. She wanted to be pissed off about it. That was her default reaction to anything she didn't understand. But Logan Maxwell intrigued her. And if his intention had been to make sure she obsessed about that kiss, well...mission accomplished.

"Got the sheets."

"Bathroom's set to rights, and I got all the samples put out," Ari announced.

Together, they stretched the fitted sheet across the mattress.

Athena wished her life wasn't in such chaos right now. Or that Logan hadn't changed things between them. If he'd still just been her wedding hookup, she could've just bounced into his bed for some stress relief. No harm, no foul.

But that wasn't what he wanted. In truth, she wasn't sure it was what she wanted either. And that was unexpected. She hadn't come home with any intention of starting anything. Her sole purpose had been to lick her wounds and make a plan for what came next. But right now, the only certainty was that she wanted to spend more time with him.

Ari smirked. "You're thinking about him."

"I'm thinking about asparagus."

The girl made a disgusted face. "Asparagus?"

"It's in season right now, and I've been pondering some new ways to fix it." Which wasn't a lie. That's what she'd been working on downstairs.

"If you're making that face over a vegetable, you've got issues, woman."

Athena laughed. "Don't knock it 'til you've tried it, kid."

They finished up the room and headed downstairs. Just in time, it seemed. She could hear Kennedy and Flynn greeting new guests as she descended.

"—Misfit Inn. We're so pleased you're here!"

"Can I just take your bag there?"

Athena's mind had already turned back to her recipes, when she spotted a familiar blond head in the foyer. "Sean?"

From where he stood by the open front door, Sean Bracelyn grinned, his teeth flashing white against the cinnamon scruff covering his cheeks. "How's my favorite goddess of the kitchen?"

Under other circumstances, she'd have been racing down the stairs and throwing herself at her old classmate for a massive hug. But that was Before. By now he was bound to know about her disgrace. Was there anybody in the cooking community who hadn't heard about it?

Apparently not content to wait for a reply, Sean strode over and picked her straight off her feet for a huge hug. "Damn, it's good to see you. It's been, what? Two years?"

Athena's bruised heart stumbled at his enthusiasm. Disgrace or no, Sean wasn't going to hold it against her. She mustered up a return embrace, pitifully happy to see a friend. "At least."

Arm slung comfortably around her shoulders, he turned back to the woman he'd come in with. She could've been a runway model, with perfect skin and all that glossy brown hair. A fitting match for Sean's golden boy looks.

Taking in Sean's besotted expression as he looked at her, Athena could only smirk. "This must be the mermaid."

He beamed and crossed over to kiss the woman's hand. "Damned straight."

The woman flashed a bemused smile. "You told her about that?"

His beard wasn't enough to hide the blush that worked its way up to his ears. "It was just a story that came out one night when we were cooking and drinking."

Highly entertained by the blush, Athena crossed her arms. "There was a metric ton of absinthe involved, as I recall."

"So. Much. Absinthe." Sean pressed a hand to his heart. "Athena, I want to introduce you to my girlfriend, Amber King. Amber, this is Athena Reynolds, one of the most talented chefs to come out of Le Cordon Bleu in the past decade. She was both friend and nemesis during my stint there."

"I think we basically kept trading the top spot the whole time."

"I'll have you know, this woman makes the best pork and prawn dumplings known to man."

Athena's lips twitched. "Yours don't suck."

"High praise, high praise." His gaze went unerringly back to Amber, who automatically leaned into him as if pulled by his gravity.

So this was the girl who'd snagged Sean's heart so long ago, without even knowing it. Athena knew from their correspondence that he'd finally snagged her back, but there was something about seeing the two of them together, all goofy grins and unhidden delight that set up an ache in her chest. Was that... envy? Not wanting to analyze that too closely, Athena moved on to a more relevant question.

"Not that it isn't great to see you, but what are you'd doing here, Sean?"

He dragged his attention back to her. "We're on vacation."

"Here?"

"Yeah! It's been on my radar since you emailed me about the opening last year. You know my siblings and I opened a resort. I figured we could compare notes."

It seemed plausible and wasn't the first time they'd discussed the possibility. And yet… "Did you know I'd be here?"

"Educated guess." There was no guile or pity in his expression, just good cheer. "I can't wait to catch up."

Athena went stiff again. Catching up meant going over all the crap she *didn't* want to talk about.

"Is their room ready?" Kennedy asked.

"Yeah. Ari and I just finished."

"Excellent. I'll just be helpin' with the luggage then," Flynn said.

As he and Amber headed out to the car,

Sean hung back. "Since you're here, I need your help with something."

Athena cast him a wary glance. "What?"

He looked back at the door and lowered his voice. "I need you to help me pull off the perfect proposal."

Ari, eavesdropping as usual, squealed. "Ohmigosh!"

Athena wrapped a hand over her mouth. "Shut it, Cupid." To Sean she said, "This is my niece Ari, our resident romantic."

Ari peeled away her hand. "I want in on helping."

"Let's let them get settled in and then we'll find time to talk about it."

Sean offered up his fist for a bump. "I'm so pumped I get to make you a part of this."

As he headed out the door himself, Athena basked in the sensation of having an ally from her world and decided this would make for a fun distraction.

CHAPTER 8

The sight of Athena's little sedan rolling down his gravel drive had Logan straightening from the tractor with a smile. She hadn't called or texted since their dinner, which he'd wondered about. But he understood she needed space to process stuff. She'd opened up more to him that night than she'd probably been comfortable with. So he'd been waiting her out, waiting until she was ready to come to him—and he hadn't expected it to be this soon. He hoped that meant she was getting more comfortable with him and the farm and not that there was more bad news. Either way, he had a proposal he hoped would intrigue her and help mitigate all the career crap she'd been dealing with.

Perhaps more than any of it, he hoped he could get his mouth on her again. He'd been thinking about that kiss, about the way she'd gone so soft and pliant in his arms, and how she'd tasted like everything that had been missing in his life. Part of him regretted stopping because he well remembered how combustible they were, how he could lose himself in the fantasy of her body. But it would be more next time, and he knew, deep down, it was the right move to wait. Nothing good could be rushed, and Logan was starting to think that whatever was brewing between them had the potential to be very, very good.

By the time she rolled to a stop in front of the barn, he'd washed the worst of the grime from his hands. Athena climbed out from the driver's side first, and at the sight of her his heart gave a quick buck in his chest. But Logan's ready smile faded when the passenger door opened and a guy stepped out. A big, muscled guy Logan had never seen before. The two of them were laughing, and Athena circled the front of the car to loop her arm through the stranger's, her head tipping to his shoulder. Everything in their body language made it clear there was some kind of intimacy between them.

A spurt of jealousy flashed through him, bright and hot. Who the hell was this guy? On the heels of that thought, he realized he didn't have a right to be jealous. He and Athena had no understanding, no formal relationship. He'd been the one to stop things from going further the other night. But none of his rationalizations did a damned thing to minimize the urge to curl his hands to fists and plow them into the other guy's face as he grinned down at Athena. Her answering grin had the heat of jealousy icing over with suspicion. Was this the infamous ex? Had he come to his senses and flown to Tennessee to grovel? Was *that* why she hadn't been in contact? Surely Athena wouldn't take him back. Not after what'd he'd done. And even if she did, what reason would she have to bring him out here?

"There's my favorite farmer! Logan, I'd like you to meet Sean Bracelyn. Sean, this is Logan Maxwell."

Logan crossed his arms before Sean could offer his hand for a shake.

If Athena noticed the deliberate snub, she didn't show it. "We need a favor."

He didn't miss the plural or the fact that she didn't release her companion. Two minutes ago he'd have been willing to give her just about anything. Now he wanted some answers first. "Yeah? What's that?"

"We need free access to your green house."

"For?"

"We come on a mission to find ingredients. I knew you'd be just the man to help us."

Sean shot her a look that couldn't be described as anything but fond. "I can't tell you how much I'm looking forward to cooking with you again."

"Same goes." Her smile flashed, quick and easy. Happy. Happier than he'd seen her since she got back to the Ridge. She turned her attention back to Logan. "I know it's no notice, but can we look around?"

He wanted to say no. He wanted an explanation. He wanted to shake her and demand to know what the fuck she was thinking taking the son of a bitch back. Acting like nothing happened.

But he did none of those things. Because Maxwells didn't make scenes. Such behavior was unseemly, and Logan prided himself on having a level head. Besides, he couldn't think of a reason to say no that wouldn't involve him proving that, when sufficiently riled, his temper was every bit a match for Athena's.

"Sure." He jerked a head toward the greenhouse. "Come on."

The two of them trailed a little bit behind him.

"So what are you thinking?" Athena asked.

"I want to hit up all the aphrodisiacs."

Logan couldn't stop his hands from balling into fists as Sean continued.

"I was talking with Meg Delaney—"

"The TV chef?"

"Yeah, I met her through my mother. She's the one who wrote that aphrodisiac cookbook, *The Food You Love*. Anyway, she had a lot of great suggestions. I'm dying to try the blood-orange roasted asparagus with blackened Anaheim peppers and pine nuts."

"I know Logan's got fabulous asparagus."

"Chocolate and strawberries for dessert, obviously. Maybe a chocolate soufflé."

"For the main, you could do roasted game hens in a fennel cream sauce," Athena added.

"Yeah, yeah, that'd be good. And pair it with a tomato, basil, and arugula salad. Basil's great for circulation and arugula has phytochemicals and antioxidants that block libido-zapping toxins."

"Oh, that's perfect." She practically purred it in a tone redolent of the one she'd used to say his name when he'd last been inside her.

Logan rounded on her. "What the hell are you doing, Athena?"

She stumbled to a halt, her eyes peeling wide. "Excuse me?"

"How the *fuck* can you take this asshole back after everything he did to you?" Logan didn't even look at Sean. "I know you regret walking away from Olympus, but is getting it back really worth being dragged back into a life that made you miserable? With a guy who treated you without a shred of respect? You're worth more than that." Didn't she understand that? Couldn't she see what he saw in her? And if she didn't, he sure as hell wanted to show her.

Color rode high in her cheeks and those usually cool gray eyes sparked with something a whole lot brighter. Logan braced himself for the storm.

Her laugh caught him like a sucker punch. It began as a chuckle that built into big, whooping guffaws that had her bending almost double.

What the actual hell?

Tears streamed down her cheeks and she

fanned her face, as if that would help her regain some control over her mirth.

"I don't consider this a laughing matter." Was that his father's stiff-necked, superior voice coming out of his mouth?

She straightened, wiping at the tears. "Sean is *not* my ex. My ex is Jayson Straker, and if you ever see me in his company again without a weapon in my hand, feel free to call out the National Guard because I've been drugged and kidnapped. No, Sean is one of my classmates from cooking school. He's here with his girlfriend on vacation, and he asked me to help him prepare the perfect proposal dinner."

"Not your ex." The blast of relief hit Logan so hard, he nearly took a step back.

Athena shook her head. "No. We never dated. We'd have killed each other."

"True story," Sean agreed.

No romantic history at all. Which meant Logan had just made a jealous ass of himself. Awesome. He finally looked at Sean. "Seems I owe you an apology."

The other man shrugged, never losing that easy cheer. "Hey, I'm glad she's got someone else watching her back. And you showed a helluva lot more restraint than I would if I got my hands on her ex."

"You don't even know the details," Athena protested.

"Don't need them."

Her expression softened. "You're a good friend, Sean."

"Damned straight. That's why you're going to help me wow my woman."

"I've seen the way she looks at you. I'm pretty sure you do that all on your own."

Finding his own equilibrium again, Logan opened the door and led them into the greenhouse. "Let's see what I can do to help with that."

Showing chefs his produce turned out to be a hugely gratifying endeavor. Their oohs and ahhhs told him they fully appreciated what he'd accomplished here in a way that everyday folks did not.

Athena looked up from some peppers she appeared to be having indecent thoughts about. "I can't believe what all you managed to cram in here. I mean, you told me some when you gave me the grand tour, but I had no idea."

"This is my laboratory, for all intents and purposes. I've spent the last couple of years experimenting, figuring out what I can grow here, when. Taking notes on how long the growth cycles are, the produce itself. The goal is to expand eventually."

"You absolutely should. Because this—" Athena gestured around them, arms wide. "—this is a chef's playground."

Maybe that was as good an entré as any. He hadn't planned to get into this with an audience, but hell, with Sean in town, who knew when she'd get back over here. Might as well put the bug in her ear.

"I've been giving some thought to that. It was something I've been wanting to talk to you about."

"Yeah? Do tell."

"Ari mentioned how you've been teaching her to cook since you've been here, and it got me thinking after you left the other day. I know it's not the haute cuisine you were trained for, but you're amazing at the whole farm-to-table cooking thing. I was thinking you could do a series of cooking classes around that theme, in conjunction with the farm."

"Me? Teach?" Athena stared at him as if the idea were ludicrous.

God, he hoped he hadn't just insulted her. "You have the time, at the moment, and you could do as many or as few as you want. Celeste Keeling—she's the head of the chamber of commerce—was really into the idea when I mentioned it to her and is full of ideas for how to promote something like that. It could be a win-win for us both."

She frowned. "The inn's kitchen isn't big enough to teach classes in."

He'd anticipated that. "No, but Crystal Blue has offered up the diner after hours as a location for the class." He'd been congratulating himself on working out all the details in advance, proving viability of concept, but as her brows drew together, Logan worried he'd overstepped his bounds by not asking her first.

"Crystal would let me back in her kitchen?"

"Back?"

"I worked there all through high school."

Well, that was yet another piece of her history he hadn't known. Logan didn't know if it was a pro or a con. Had they parted on bad terms? Crystal hadn't said anything to that effect. Too late to back out now. "Either way, it'd be good publicity for the farm and the inn as sponsor. And I think maybe you'd enjoy it," he finished, feeling lame. "It's just an idea. Nothing's set in stone. I just thought I'd put it out there as something for you to consider." Why hadn't he waited until they were alone to bring this up?

"I'll think about it." Her words were slow, reluctant.

Logan didn't know her well enough to be certain whether that meant no, yes, or if he should take the statement at face value. But at this point, he'd pushed his luck as much as he dared. "No rush."

He was used to feeling confident with Athena. Of knowing the right way to handle her. But in the span of half an hour, he'd proved he didn't know her anywhere near as well as he'd thought. He hadn't been able to tell old friend from ex. He hadn't known about her history with Crystal. And he didn't know how to read her reaction to his idea. Talk about a reality check. But he wanted to know all those things. He wanted to know everything about her, and his own impatience surprised him.

Squashing his frustration, he stepped past them both and gestured toward the back corner of the greenhouse. "I don't have any blood oranges, but I do have these dwarf oranges."

"OKAY, we're alone. Are we gonna talk about the elephant in the kitchen?" Sean asked.

I'd rather cook the elephant. Athena unpacked the bounty they'd scored at Logan's farm. "You're a Bracelyn. I thought your family's whole schtick was pretending stuff didn't happen."

"Only if you're another Bracelyn. Which you're not, so spill, woman."

She grimaced. But Sean had once been one of her closest friends. If she couldn't discuss this with him, who *could* she talk to? "It's mortifying."

"Why?"

"I secretly dated my boss, who then turned around and slept with my sous chef. During service. Is there some variation on this that *isn't* mortifying?"

His mouth fell open, his good humor fading. "Damn. *That's* why you went after Jayson with a knife? I knew there was more to the whole thing than what's circulating."

Athena winced. "Do I even want to know what's circulating?"

"Nothing that won't be replaced by the next

big scandal."

Yeah, who knew when or what that would be or what damage her reputation would sustain in the meantime. "I know you *mean* that to be comforting. But I'm seriously worried, Sean. Why would anyone want to take a chance on me after all that?"

"Because you're a damned fine chef. One very publicized emotional outburst doesn't change that. You're hardly the first chef to lose her shit in the kitchen. We're a passionate breed. Hell, Gordon Ramsay's made a freaking career out of having temper tantrums on camera."

"And he can get away with it because he's a guy. Female chefs get crucified all the time for the exact same shit that male chefs get away with constantly."

"Okay, I won't deny there's a double standard. I just don't think this is as big a deal to the rest of the world as it feels to you being in the middle of it. But anyway, I wasn't asking about what happened with your ex. I was talking about the sparks shooting between you and Logan. Dude was ready to grind my bones to make his bread because he thought I'd hurt you. What's going on there?"

Oh, that. Suddenly, discussing life's worst and most embarrassing moment seemed more appealing than discussing attractive farmers. "I don't know."

He leveled her with some serious side eye.

"No really, I don't know." And she'd love some clarification. "We had a...thing at Kennedy's wedding last year."

"I love things at weddings. That's where Amber and I finally got together. There were some exploding chafing dishes at the reception and meatball carnage, and we had to try to save her dress..." Catching Athena's smirk, he cleared his throat. "Anyway. You had a thing at Kennedy's wedding. Was it good?"

She went brows up. "Falling in love has turned you into a girl."

"It is my God-given right as your friend to

give you shit. Besides, I'm not asking for all the details, just in general."

"What do you want me to say?" she demanded. "The earth moved? I saw stars?" All true. Chemistry most certainly wasn't a problem between them.

"Given the way your hackles are up, I'm gonna guess that's accurate. What happened between last summer and now?"

Pressing her mouth together, she blew out a frustrated breath. "Nothing came of it. He was here, I was in Chicago. I didn't see him again until just before Christmas, and by then I was with Jayson."

"May he rot in hell," Sean intoned, moving around her with an ease and familiarity established back in their cooking school days.

Athena lifted the fennel in toast. "Hear, hear."

"You're not with Jayson now."

"No." She'd reached a point where that fact relieved her. "But I'm not with Logan either."

Sean's brows drew together. "Because you

don't want to be? Because that guy is clearly not an unbiased party when it comes to you."

You're worth more than that.

Logan's eyes had been ripe with fury as he'd said it, and she wasn't above admitting—to herself at least—that seeing him angry on her behalf had turned her on. When was the last time someone who wasn't family had defended her? Looked out for her? Maybe never. Athena had always been fine with that. She valued her independence and had learned early on to take care of herself. But he'd been…magnificent. If they'd been alone, she might have tried again to finish what she'd started last week. But he hadn't gone there, despite the fact that she'd made it clear that's what she'd wanted.

Restless and unsettled, she jerked her shoulders and began prepping the game hens. "Because…I don't know. I thought we could do something casual again but that's not what he wants, and I'm not in a place to consider anything more serious, even if I knew whether I wanted that. Which I don't."

Liar.

"Worried about rebound?"

"Yeah. That and I have no idea where I'll end up next. It seems pointless to start something here when my next job is bound to be elsewhere." Yet hadn't that kiss started something? She hadn't been able to stop thinking about it, about him. He'd made her *yearn,* damn him. For something she couldn't quite put a name to. Or didn't want to.

"The next job doesn't have to be at the ends of the earth. You could do what I did. Open a restaurant here as part of the inn. I've loved having my own place and working with my family."

"You aren't the first one to mention that. But our little inn and spa is a far cry from the luxury resort you and your siblings opened. We don't target the same kind of clientele. We're doing remarkably well, but we just started the second phase expansion of the spa. We can't afford another expansion for a restaurant." She understood better than her sisters the cost of starting one from scratch. Their well-intentioned offer wasn't a financial reality.

"What about Logan's idea? The cooking classes? There are plenty of places where cooking schools are a part of the vacation experience. Hell, even guest chefs. I'm working on talking Meg into coming to the resort for a sexy couples retreat weekend centered around her cookbook. Lots of people would jump at being taught by a Michelin-starred chef."

Athena froze, a flush of shame sweeping over her like the backwash of heat from a flambéed dessert. Not meeting his eyes, she kept her hands steady as she spatchcocked the hens. "There's only one of those in this kitchen."

"What are you talking about?"

"They stripped me of my star."

A knife clattered against the counter and Sean's big hands curved around her shoulders, turning her to face him. "What happened?"

The automatic concern and warmth in his eyes had heat stinging the back of hers. Sucking in a breath for fortitude, she let it all spill out.

By the time she'd finished, the kitchen was full of the scents of roasting meat, blackened peppers, and the chocolate that would be the base for the soufflé.

"I don't know what happened. I just...when my mother died, something in me simply stopped working. I stopped caring. Everything I'd worked for suddenly seemed less important. Looking back, if I hadn't been still raw from grief, I probably never would've gone for Jayson in the first place. It was months after the funeral, but I just...wasn't processing. Wasn't letting myself, I guess. He got to me in a weak moment, helping to pick up the load that had gotten too heavy."

It hurt to admit that. To realize she'd chosen him out of weakness because she'd been feeling needy. Oh God. Was that what she was doing with Logan?

"There's nothing wrong with needing support and comfort. It's shitty that he used that against you. Shittier that it meant the loss of something important to you. But the stars aren't the be-all-end-all in this business."

Athena quirked her lips. "Right. Because we're breaking our necks and working our asses off slaving for that recognition just for fun?"

"No really. And, let's be honest. The stars go to the restaurant, not the chefs. The chefs are the heart of it, but it's the whole package. They didn't strip Olympus's star until you were gone."

"We both know that decision was probably made before I left. Most likely due to inconsistent performance over months."

"So what? Yeah, it sucks. And you have every right to be upset about it. And not to beat a dead horse, but Gordon Ramsay cried when The London lost its two-star rating. But it didn't ruin him and there's no reason to let it ruin you. One bad year is not going to ruin your career."

Athena snapped the woody stem off a spear of asparagus with perhaps more force than necessary. "I don't have Ramsay's other achievements to back me up. Right now, I've got a lost star and a viral video of my worst kitchen meltdown ever. I don't want to set up some cooking classes only to have a bunch of Lookie Lous coming to gawk at me."

"Is that the only objection you've got to teaching? Because you're worried about being judged for that video?"

"It's not just that, although that's a big part of it. You know me, Sean. I don't exactly people well."

"You've been teaching your niece."

"She's different. She's a kid, and she loves me."

"But you've enjoyed teaching her?"

She'd enjoyed the hell out of it. Ari was enthusiastic and just loved spending quality time with her family. "Sure. It's not like the competitive kitchens we came up in. She legit wants to learn. No ego. No end game."

"I think your Logan is right. You probably would enjoy teaching normal people how to elevate their food. You hated those hoity toity assholes who flocked to Olympus. Why not try the classes? Set up some kind of short run sort of deal while you're trying to figure out your options?"

"Maybe I will." It'd be something different to try anyway. "And he's not my Logan."

Of course Ari came sailing in on the heels of that statement. "But he wants to be!"

She didn't quail one iota in the face of Athena's flat stare. Instead, she turned to Sean. "Your lady is massaged, rubbed, and buffed to within an inch of her life. She's currently upstairs getting ready for your evening. Dinner is still at six?"

"That is the plan."

"Then you'd best hop to so you can finish readying your part."

Athena waved him on. "Go. I've got the rest of this. I'll put the finishing touches on everything, and it'll be all ready for you to serve."

Sean's eyes went wide and his cheeks paled a bit beneath the scruff of his beard. "Shit, this is it, isn't it?" He wiped his hands on his apron.

"It is. You're gonna wow her."

"What if she says no?"

"She's not gonna say no," Ari assured him. "She just spent all day telling everybody at the spa how amazing you are."

"Okay." He stripped the apron off and nodded. "Okay." He swept Athena into a tight hug. "Thanks for helping with all this. It means a lot."

"Anytime. And thanks for listening."

"Always. You're gonna figure this out."

"I sure as hell hope so. Now shoo. Go get ready."

But he hesitated, looking over the food and muttering. "It has to be *perfect.*"

"It will be perfect. Now go on, get out of here. Knock her socks off."

"Any last-second advice?"

She couldn't help it. She doubled over laughing with incredulity. "You're looking to *me* for love advice? I'm sorry, where were you during the entire discussion of my disaster of a love life today?"

"Not love advice, exactly. *Proposal* advice. You're a woman."

"Last time I checked."

Sean glanced toward the door to the dining room. "I thought about slipping the ring in her champagne glass but—"

"Ugh, no." Athena made a face, thinking of how often that trite move had been pulled at Olympus. "You can do better than that. Besides, isn't that a Dom Perignon Chef De Cave Limited Edition you brought?"

"Yeah."

"You don't go sticking jewelry in two-hundred dollar a bottle champagne."

"Is getting down on one knee too old school?"

That mental image did something funny to her insides. Ari would say she was going gooey, a fact which Athena would deny until her dying day. "Definitely not," she said briskly. "That's romantic. And sweet."

"And it puts me eye level with her rack," Sean pointed out.

There went the gooey feeling. Athena whacked him with a pot holder. "You're such a *guy*. Get out of my kitchen. *Now.*"

With a grin, Sean scurried off.

Ari heaved a blissful sigh. "Damn, they're cute."

"They really are. Is everything else ready?"

"And waiting. I just need to light the candles. The champagne is already chilled. And I'm all set to play server."

Athena hooked an arm around her shoulders. "You did good, kid. Want to help me finish this up?"

Ari brightened. "Yeah!"

She paid ruthless attention as Athena walked her through the final finishing touches on the various dishes. If everybody was as enthusiastic and compliant as her niece, Athena thought she really would enjoy teaching cooking classes. The idea of it continued to roll around her brain as they plated and prepped.

By the time the entrée had been carried out, she'd made her decision.

Ari came back into the kitchen, backed by sounds of pleasure over the food that were one step above pornographic.

"Obviously the food is going over well," Athena said.

"Unquestionably." Ari looked over the extra still spread over the counter. "You know, there's enough food here for an army." She slanted a glance at Athena. "Farmers get awfully hungry."

Athena shot her the side eye. "Smart ass."

"You know sometimes he eats Hungry Man dinners."

"Bring me the basket."

CHAPTER 9

*A*fter Athena and Sean left, Logan spent the rest of the afternoon second-guessing himself, thinking about all the ways he could've handled—well, everything—better.

He'd tipped his hand and showed far too much with that outburst about her ex. Not that it wasn't a hundred percent truth, but she'd said she wasn't up for anything serious. Maybe he'd been nudging her in that direction, but he'd been taking his time about it, letting her warm up to the idea. Maybe that plan would've worked in the long game. But that, in combination with the whole cooking school idea, might as well have been an announcement of, "Hey, I want you to stay and I figured out exactly how you can." Which it was. But Athena wasn't a woman who liked being told what to do. He *knew* that about her. And if he hadn't been so rattled by thinking she'd taken her ex back, he probably could've—would've—waited until he could just slip it into the conversation more casually, so she thought the whole thing was her idea.

Too late now.

By the time he made it into the shower, he was convinced he'd blown the whole damned thing. It left him feeling panicky and pissed. Haunted by the should've, would've, could'ves, the sharp edge of something that might've been grief lodged in his throat.

Get a fucking grip, Maxwell. You don't know that it's over.

As he scrubbed off layers of dirt and grease and sweat, he considered damage control. How was he going to salvage this situation? *Was* it salvageable? Should he apologize? Or would talking about it further just make the whole situation worse? Maybe he should just wait and let her process, come to him in her own time, even if that was to say no. His review of the options was cut short as he stepped out of the shower and heard a clatter from the kitchen.

Oh hell.

Bo and Peep had gotten into the garbage again. He really thought the motion-activated trash can with the auto-locking top would stop that crap, but the pair of them were so smart, they'd probably figured out how to tag team it. Tucking a towel around his hips, he jogged downstairs, determined to shoo them outside before they could make any more of a mess.

But it wasn't Bo and Peep in his kitchen. It was Athena.

Her hair was bundled in a messy knot and the soft, over-sized t-shirt she wore slipped partly off one shoulder as she turned. "Hey, I—"

At the sight of him, her eyes went dark as smoke and her lips parted on an indrawn breath. Her gaze scraped over him, firm as a touch, and the expression of absolute hunger had him going hard in an instant.

Gripping the edge of the towel, Logan struggled for some control. Looking past her, he noticed the containers of food spread out on the counter. "You brought dinner."

Knowing she communicated in food, he tried to figure out what that meant. A détente? A yes? A way to let him down gently? He was too busy salivating over her to find an answer.

Hissing out a breath, she snapped the top back on some kind of salad and crossed the room. "It can wait."

Her mouth and hands were on him before he could blink, ravenous, insatiable. Whatever blood was left in his brain drained south.

"Athena," he gasped against her kiss. He should slow this down. Stop her so they could talk about—everything. But her hands felt so damned good against his bare skin.

"Don't say no, Logan. Please don't say no this time."

There was that please again. It absolutely slayed his resistance.

Dragging her against him, he devoured her mouth with matching fervor. With the press of her body, she edged him back, toward the living room and the sofa. But Logan wanted her in his bed. Needed her there, where he'd imagined her so many times.

Gripping her legs, he boosted her up until she wrapped them around his hips, dislodging the towel in the process, so she was settled directly on his erection. He swayed, considering for a moment just pressing her against the nearest wall. But her jeans were in the way and that wasn't what he wanted. She deserved better. Finding his balance, he surged up the stairs, managing not to drop her. Turning blindly down the hall, he staggered into his room and tumbled her onto the bed.

She bounced once, her eyes roaming over his naked form. "God, you're beautiful."

"That's my line." Then he was on her again,

helping her strip out of her clothes with a swift efficiency that bordered on desperation.

He'd wanted to go slow, to cherish her. To show her the tenderness she didn't seem to think she needed. But she was a living flame in his arms, and everything in her touch, her kiss, urged him to hurry, hurry. It wasn't in him to deny her.

When she was naked, he dragged her to the edge of the bed and lowered his mouth to feast. She bucked beneath him, gasping a creative patois of curses in at least three languages, even as she gripped his hair to hold him to her. He ruthlessly drove her to flashpoint, then continued to lick and suck, drawing out every last pulse of pleasure from her release, until she tugged at his hair again.

"You. Now."

As he reached for a condom in the night-stand drawer, he wondered if that was her head chef voice. The absolute command in it was sexy as hell.

She yanked the packet out of his hand and

ripped it open, rolling the condom on and stroking him from base to tip, until his eyes rolled back in his head.

Oh, hell no. There was only so much control he was willing to cede. Curling his hands around her wrists, he pressed them into the bed and rose over her, settling between her thighs, his cock just nudging her entrance. He held there, staring down at her, drinking in the desire in every line of her face and body as he struggled to find some control, some finesse.

But Athena would have none of it. Wrapping those long, long legs around him, she arched up and pulled him inside in one fast, hard thrust.

They both cried out.

"Athena." Her name was all he could manage as her body tightened around him, a remembered perfection that had haunted him for nearly a year.

"Don't stop," she gasped.

He couldn't if his life depended on it.

She didn't want slow and sweet. Not now.

Promising he'd give that to her later, he began to move, setting a merciless pace that drove them both up. Her body rose and fell with every stroke of his, matching and challenging him to go faster, harder, until he forgot everything but the slick heat of her body. As he felt the first flutters of her orgasm begin to ripple around him, he gave himself over to it, to her, and let the heat consume them both.

THE LAST DYING rays of the sun slanted through the blinds, gilding the caramel-colored walls and the skin of the man slumped over her. Sleepy, sated, Athena decided it was a helluva view. At some point during the main event, Logan had shifted from holding her wrists down to threading his fingers with hers. They were still laced together, and he was still inside her, his face pressed into her throat. His heart thudded dully against hers, a strangely comforting echo of her own racing pulse. Normally, she wanted space after sex, not cuddles. But she wasn't in any hurry for him to move.

As she lay sweaty and exhausted, still pinned beneath him, she realized the power of her own self-delusion. In her months with Jayson, she'd convinced herself things in the bedroom had been good, that she'd been getting regular, excellent orgasms. But she'd been fooling herself.

Holy hell.

Logan had been amazing at Opal Springs. A playful, generous lover, who'd been exactly what she'd needed to chase away the grief that had accompanied the first family wedding without her mother. But she'd convinced herself that she'd romanticized it, making the whole experience better than it had been because she couldn't really have him.

She'd been wrong. Completely, unutterably wrong.

She'd known being with Logan again would be good. Their chemistry had never been in question. But this...this had been...explosive. Full of pent-up passion and a need that somehow transcended the physical. One that, now she'd had him again, only felt keener.

And that scared the shit out of her.

As if sensing her shift in mood, Logan roused himself, lifting up enough to look into her face. As his hazel eyes searched hers, she wanted to curl in on herself. She felt exposed, as if he could see into her, to all the weaknesses and vulnerabilities she tried to pretend she didn't have.

Without releasing her hands, he brushed his lips over hers. "Tell me you're not going to run away now."

Her fingers flexed in his, wanting to push him away, to hide, because part of her did want to run. "This wasn't why I came over here."

His lips quirked. "Wasn't it?"

At the amusement in his voice, she scowled. "You distracted me. With your abs and your towel." God, she still wanted to trace the lines of his six pack with her tongue. Later. There'd be a later now, for sure.

He grinned full-on at that. "If that's what it

takes to get you into my bed, I'll make it my standard uniform."

Confused by his playfulness, she frowned. "You had the chance to get me into your bed before. You didn't take it."

One hand gently stroked through her tangled hair. "You weren't really here for me then. You were tonight. On some level, anyway. You brought me dinner."

He sounded way too pleased by that. "Sean and I made too much food. I thought you deserved some for helping us out today." And, okay, yeah, maybe she had wanted to test out those aphrodisiac recipes for herself. But they hadn't even touched the food yet.

He kissed her again—the kind of kiss that said he wasn't through with her yet—and rolled off, padding into the bathroom to take care of business. Over the sound of running water he called, "Did she say yes?"

Still feeling exposed, Athena grabbed up one of his shirts from a hamper that looked liked clean laundry and slipped it on. "So fast, I'm not sure they even made it to the chocolate soufflé."

"Good for Sean." Logan padded back into the bedroom, sliding his arms around her waist and trapping her hands against his chest. "I *am* sorry I thought he was your ex. He seems like a good guy."

"He is a good guy." Athena waited a moment to see if he'd continue with the apologies. "You're not going to apologize for getting all in my face about it?"

He sobered. "It's how I feel. You deserve so much better than you got. I couldn't just stand by when I thought you were making a mistake."

Scowling, she thumped him on the shoulder. "I'm still a little pissed at you for thinking I'd take Jayson back. I'm not that stupid."

"I'll apologize for that. It was the jealousy talking."

Appeased and wanting to lighten the mood, Athena smirked. "I suppose I'll forgive you, if only because jealousy looks good on you."

Logan didn't take the cue. "Look, Athena, I know you aren't looking for anything serious."

She tensed. Why was he doing this? Why did they have to define things right now? They'd had sex. Stupendous sex. Sex she really hoped they'd have again. Soon. Couldn't they just leave it at that?

But he was still talking. "I won't lie to you that I am hoping for the serious. It's how I'm wired. But I won't push you. I know your life is in upheaval right now, and you're not ready to make any decisions."

His pause felt pregnant with quintuplets. He was making too many concessions to what he actually wanted.

"I feel like there's another 'But' hanging out in there."

His hands laced behind her back, pulling her closer against his still gloriously naked body. But it didn't quite distract her from the serious-ness of his expression. "I'm willing to roll with the casual because now that I've had you again, once isn't going to be enough. But I've got one major requirement. As long as we're getting naked together, we're not getting naked with anybody else. I don't share."

Some of the tension leeched out of her. "I can live with that."

Smiling, he bent to rub his nose against hers.

Athena stared up at him, flummoxed. "Did you…just give me Eskimo kisses?"

"I can fondle your butt if it'd make you feel better," he offered.

"It might." That, at least, made sense to her.

He slid his palms over her backside, then back up again beneath the tail of the shirt until he cupped one cheek in each hand and squeezed. "There. Are you ready to show me what you brought for dinner?"

"A meal that, if it does its job, will make your putting clothes on again completely superfluous."

"I like the sound of that."

She cleaned up and they headed downstairs, where she began warming the food.

"It was better fresh."

"I'm sure it'll be amazing either way." Logan, sadly having donned a pair of jeans, slid his hands over her hips and nibbled at the juncture of her neck and shoulder. "So was dinner the only reason you came by?"

Athena shivered, bobbling the spear of asparagus she was trying to plate. "No. I came to talk about your cooking school proposal."

His lips stilled and he straightened, turning her to face him. "It was just an idea. I didn't intend to pressure you or make you feel like I wanted to use your celebrity to my benefit."

The idea of that almost made her smile. Almost. "I think you grossly overestimate my celebrity. Notoriety maybe." Because that thought did too much to dim the buzz of arousal she had going on, Athena shook it off. "But no. I think it's actually a good idea."

"You do?" His genuine surprise bemused her. She was so used to seeing his easy confidence.

"I'm not ready to make any major career decisions. I don't have any kind of offers to even entertain right now. For better or worse, I need to lay low while the scandal blows over. This allows me to do that and still cook, which I need to do to stay sane. And—" She skimmed her fingers over his bare chest. "I hope it means you and I will be spending more time together."

"As much as you want. Naked or otherwise." He caught her hand and stilled it over his heart. "There's something here, Athena. We didn't get a chance to explore it before, and maybe right now is crap circumstances, but I think we owe it to ourselves to see what it is."

She didn't know what she'd do if he was right, if this turned out to be more than a casual affair. Her next career move wouldn't be here. She knew that much. But that was a problem for another day. She'd hit her max of what she was capable of handling.

"How about we start with the food and go from there?"

He smiled. "Sounds good to me."

CHAPTER 10

On the Friday before Memorial Day, the long, wooded drive down to The Misfit Inn was already lined with vehicles. People were headed toward the house with coolers hauled between them, camp chairs over shoulders, and picnic blankets tucked under arms. Logan could already hear the musicians tuning up out back for the inaugural performance of the season. For something that had been impromptu entertainment last summer during Flynn's initial stay, Jam Night had become The Place To Be on Friday night in Eden's

Ridge as soon as the evenings turned warm. Local musicians from near and far gathered together for a few hours of improvised music, and the townsfolk and guests made a party of it. Logan had enjoyed the hell out of the ones he'd attended.

But as he made his way down the crushed-gravel drive, unfamiliar nerves skated over his skin, like that time during his sophomore year of high school, when he showed up at Homecoming with Anna Beth Alton in the wake of her dumping the most popular guy in their class. Stupid to feel that mix of excitement and dread, but there it was. The wondering how everybody would react. Because he was with Athena now. Except, he'd promised to roll with the casual, and he had no idea what she'd told her family about them or how he was supposed to treat her in public.

Circling around to the grassy space behind the house and spa, where the stage had been set up—really just strands of cafe lights strung up in rows over the patch of lawn where the musicians had clustered their own chairs—he looked for his woman.

His woman. He liked the sound of that a helluva lot. He wondered if Athena went for a little caveman possessiveness.

Flynn caught his eye and lifted a hand in a wave. Logan jerked his head in acknowledgment, but continued to scan the clusters of people, searching for Athena. Not finding her, he headed into the house.

She was, of course, in the kitchen, her hair put up in one of those messy buns. He wanted to kiss her nape, watch her shiver before taking all that tawny hair down and losing his hands in it. But there were people everywhere, including a huge chunk of her family.

"Now don't get mad." Kennedy held up her hands in peace.

Uh oh. Logan quietly shut the door behind him, so as not to interrupt.

Athena glanced his way before turning her attention back to her sister, arms crossed. "You realize that prefacing anything with that statement automatically primes me to do exactly that, right?"

"It's a good thing," Kennedy promised.

Athena just narrowed her eyes and waited. Logan edged his way around the kitchen toward her, ready to intervene or mediate should the need arise.

"It's just that Celeste and I put together a website advertising the cooking school."

"And?"

"Well, we attached it to the inn's website and the chamber of commerce. It just went live day before yesterday."

"Like we talked about. Again, not seeing what it is I'm not supposed to get mad about. Unless you used the video."

"No, of course not. It's just—we had the booking system already live, so we could test and make sure it worked right before doing the big advertising push. Athena, the whole series is already sold out."

Athena's expression froze. "What do you mean already sold out? How can you even have a series? I haven't decided what I'm teaching yet."

"We set it up as to be determined. You said you wanted four weeks, one class a week. We didn't think it would fill up that fast. But how awesome is that? Less than forty-eight hours and just on your name alone! It's proof this was a great idea."

A muscle ticked in her jaw. "And when is this first class allegedly supposed to be?"

Kennedy winced and Logan automatically took a step closer to Athena. "Next week."

"Next week! How am I supposed to be ready to teach classes next week? I haven't got a menu, we haven't figured out the logistics of setting up cooking stations—"

"Actually, we have. We're borrowing all the hot plates from the home ec class at the high school," Pru interrupted.

"Hot plates." Athena breathed the word like a curse and passed a hand over her face.

Her shoulders bunched as she struggled to hold on to her emotions. Logan wondered if anybody else realized it was fear, not temper, that was simmering. Edging into her space, he kept his voice low. "Take a minute and breathe."

Her eyes snapped to his, and he could see she was drowning, panic and fury warring for dominance. Logan couldn't stand it. Taking a risk, he tugged her in to comfort and calm. Expecting her to lash out, he was almost as surprised as everybody else when she wrapped her arms around him and snuggled in, pressing her face to his shoulder.

"Next week," she whimpered, her voice muffled against his chest.

Logan kissed the top of her head. "You'll do just fine. Come out to the farm tomorrow. We'll go through the fields, see what's peaking. Once you know what you have to work with, you'll be fine. That's a big part of farm-to-table, right? Rolling with whatever's fresh."

She nodded but didn't look up.

"You can test whatever you want. We'll get you some guinea pigs," he promised.

"I'd probably do better with your pigs than

the people."

He tipped her chin up so she had to look at him. "It'll be fine."

Holding his gaze, she inhaled a long breath and let it back out. "It'll be fine." She didn't sound convinced.

"It'll be fine because you are a badass chef. Say it."

"Seriously?" When he just arched a brow in expectation she sighed. "I am a badass chef."

"Damn straight."

He felt some of the tension drain out of her. She popped up to her toes to brush a kiss over his cheek. "Thanks, Farmer Boy."

When she let him go, everybody was staring, which told Logan everything he needed to know. Athena likely hadn't filled them in about squat. Well, they'd have to be told something now.

Ignoring them all, as if the subject of the cooking school was closed, she hefted a tray and nodded to Ari. "C'mon. We've got apps to serve."

Not bothering to hide her Cheshire Cat grin, Ari grabbed the second tray of hors d'oeuvres and followed.

As soon as the door closed behind them, Kennedy managed to pick her jaw up off the floor. "Who is that and what did she do with my sister?"

"Dude, you're, like, the Athena Whisperer. I don't think I'd have believed it if I hadn't just seen it," Xander said.

Logan resisted the urge to shoot him the bird. Barely. "Don't be a jackass. This whole project stresses her out."

Pru settled on one of the bar stools and folded both hands over her belly as she studied him. "You're good for her."

He'd have felt better if she said it with some kind of a smile rather than that neutral, assessing look that set up an itch between his shoulder blades. Was this what his clients had felt like back in grad school? "Then why don't you sound entirely happy about that?"

"I'm just worried about what happens down

the line."

He heard the unspoken, "when she leaves."

He'd thought about that. Of course, he had. But if he'd waited until things were settled, he wouldn't be a part of the decision to stay or go. He wouldn't have a shot. At least this way, he'd factor in. Hopefully as a weight on the "stay" side of the scales.

"I've just got to be patient and hope things work out. Hope and patience are kinda the watch words of a farmer."

"Well, I for one am pulling for you," Kennedy said. "She's...I don't know. Softer, somehow, around you."

"Oh God," Xander said, "don't let her hear *that*."

Did none of them understand the gooey marshmallow center beneath that prickly exterior? He started to say something, then thought better of it. Athena had been vulnerable with him. She trusted him. If she didn't feel the same ease with her family, it wasn't his place to intervene.

"We'll see." Logan jerked his head toward the door and music that had started up. "I'm gonna go find a spot to listen."

Outside, he swung by the drink station and plucked a beer out of the big, iced bucket of drinks. The music was lively, with a bluegrass edge tonight. The lawn was covered with people, some familiar, some not. He'd been in Eden's Ridge for nearly six years now, and it continued to amaze him that there were new people to meet in a town this small. Then again, everything seemed small compared to his hometown of Memphis.

Skirting the edges of the crowd, he found a tree to prop up and watched Athena circulate, offering appetizers from her tray, exchanging brief moments of conversation with people enjoying her food. She wasn't as bad with people as she thought she was. When it was the food being judged instead of her, she was in her element. Confident and in control. Logan thought about what she'd told him about her father, about what it was like growing up in the wake of his overdose. Something like that cast a helluva long shadow. Would her professional woes be just as bad?

Lost in thought, he didn't notice her approach until a hand snaked around his waist from behind and a lithe body pressed itself against his back. "Want to get out of here, away from the crowd?"

Logan's body stirred. She'd said the same thing last summer at Kennedy's wedding. He didn't have to be asked twice. Without a word, he laced his fingers with hers and they melted into the darkness, skirting the perimeter of the property until they found the trail down to Opal Springs.

As they picked their way down the path, the music and voices muted.

"This feels delightfully familiar," he observed.

"I've had an itch to come back here with you," she admitted. "This was the first real opportunity."

"I can't count the number of times I thought

about that night. About wanting a repeat. About wanting you."

"What a difference a year makes, huh?" In the faint trickle of moonlight through the trees, he caught the flash of her smile.

"Why did you pick me last year?" He hadn't meant to ask it and regretted the words when she stumbled. He reached out to steady her. "You don't have to answer."

"No, it's fine. It's a reasonable question." She took her time, waiting until they'd made it to the water's edge to answer. Because she needed that long to gather her thoughts? Or because the springs felt like the place for secrets and whispers?

"I liked you. We have chemistry. And, honestly, I wanted a distraction. Kennedy's wedding was…hard. I'm happy for her and Xander both, thrilled they finally sorted out their crap. But the whole thing just felt a little hollow for me because Mom wasn't there to see it. I needed something to chase away the bittersweet. You more than fit the bill."

"I enjoyed the hell out of being your distraction."

He'd hoped his sincerity would make her smile. But her expression was sober as she turned to face him. "It started out that way this time, too. I was hurting and I wanted to forget for a while. I came back to you. And that was an asshole thing to do."

"Athena—"

"No, listen. I've been thinking about this, and I need to get it out. I came back to you for selfish reasons. I thought I could be okay with that, with doing the whole casual sex thing, whenever, wherever we wanted."

A tendril of panic slithered through Logan's system. Had she brought him all the way down here to break things off? "What are you saying?"

"That even though that's where we started, with the casual, it's more than that. You're more than a distraction. I need you to know that. To know that I'm not...using you. You were right when you said there's something here."

Relief had his knees going loose, all the

ready fight draining out of him. She wasn't going to make him fight to convince her. Instead she'd given him a gift, acknowledging the weight of what was between them. It was more than he'd dared hope for yet. Maybe that meant things were already swinging in his favor. Maybe he already had more weight on the stay side of the scales than he'd thought. That uncharacteristic impatience reared up, urging him to talk, to share, to plan for the possible future that felt just out of reach. But he held it in because he understood this was as much as she could handle right now.

He stroked a thumb down the parallel lines between her brows. "That worries you."

"I don't know what to do with this. With you."

"There's time to figure it out." He'd done everything he could to make sure there was. Wanting to lighten the mood, give her some of that distraction she craved, he pulled her in. "And I've got a few ideas about how we can use it."

Lowering his head, he captured her smile with a kiss.

ATHENA DIDN'T KNOW what she'd expected, stepping into the diner kitchen for the first time in nearly a decade. She felt like an entirely different woman from the girl who'd worked here. But the diner had changed little. The same ancient grill and commercial range had been scrubbed to gleaming, and the worn tile floors still showed the tracks of years of the dance between counter and range and walk-in cooler. A faint scent of grease lingered beneath the sharp bite of lemon cleaner. It smelled like home. In high school, this had been one of her sanctuaries. At Crystal's elbow, she'd honed her natural culinary skills sharp enough to land her a spot in her first high-end kitchen in London. From there she'd cooked her way across Europe until she earned her way into Chef Ossani's kitchen —her gateway to Le Cordon Bleu. After high school, she'd left here for Europe, full of hopes and dreams and drive, so relieved to be escaping this small town, where she'd felt judged. She'd gone to prove herself. And she had. But after everything that had happened, this return felt more like disgrace than triumph.

The door to the dining room opened. Crystal swung through it, leading with her generous hips. "You're here!" The older woman beamed at her, wiping hands on the towel tucked into her apron.

"I am." Athena wondered if Crystal could hear the nerves. "Thank you for letting us host the cooking school here."

"I'm just pleased as punch to have you back in my kitchen. I knew you were destined for big things, and here you are, a famous chef, sharing your knowledge with us common folk. I'm just so proud of you!" Crystal bustled across the kitchen to envelop Athena in a coffee-scented hug that she didn't know what to do with.

Athena's throat went thick. Crystal had been another sort-of mother to her growing up. And maybe she hadn't really realized that until right this second, when she was missing Joan so damned much it hurt. So she resisted her first urge to put distance between them to regain control of her emotions and opted for the truth.

"I don't know if I ever said it back then, so I'm saying it now. Thank you for giving me the opportunity to work here, for being there for me growing up. You were a big part of my success. In giving me my foundation."

"Oh!" She gave a mighty sniff and squeezed Athena again. "I always considered you one of mine."

Had Athena realized that as a teenager? She'd been so wound up about feeling like an outsider, sometimes even with her sisters, she'd lived life with shields up all the time. That had been standard operating procedure since...well, always. What else had she missed because she was too busy protecting herself?

Eyes prickling, she awkwardly wrapped her arms around Crystal.

The bell above the diner's front door

jingled.

"That's probably my first students."

Crystal patted her back and released her. "You go on out there and greet people."

People. Yay.

But Athena wiped damp palms against her pants and pushed through the door as ordered.

It wasn't students. Not yet. It was Logan balancing two huge boxes of produce from the farm. Athena's mood lifted at the sight of him. Ari trailed in his wake with one more box.

"Hey gorgeous. You ready for this?" He looked calm and steady and unflappable as usual. Did he have any idea how appealing that was?

Behind him, Ari beamed, her little cupid heart clearly fluttering on overdrive.

Athena couldn't handle that on top of everything else, so she firmly turned away from her niece to focus on Logan's question. "Not even close. But we're here, so I'll muddle through."

He set the boxes on one of the tables that had been rearranged to make two long rows of work stations and slid a hand around her waist. "You're going to be brilliant."

The lingering kiss he laid on her did a lot more to settle her nerves than his words.

"I'm just gonna go help Crystal in the kitchen," Ari sang.

"Take your time," Logan murmured.

Athena hooked her fingers through his belt loops. "Are we sure we have to do this? I can think of way more rewarding ways to spend our afternoon."

"You won't seduce me out of this. But I'll happily seduce you after."

"Promise?"

"Cross my heart. By the time this is through, you'll have earned a very thorough reward."

The fresh hum in her blood muted the anxiety a little. She'd been finding out exactly how thorough Logan could be.

"I'm holding you to that."

He grinned, slow and wicked. "Yes, Chef."

In all her years cooking, Athena had never imagined seducing anyone in her kitchen. After walking in on Mari and Jayson, she hadn't imagined she ever would. But looking up at Logan Maxwell, with his farm-made good looks and sexy smile, she thought she might change her mind. It might be extremely gratifying to give him orders and have him jump to do her bidding…

"Are you ready to finish setting up the stations?"

Flushing, Athena stepped back and didn't quite meet Crystal's gaze. "Yeah, we should put out ingredients."

As she, Logan, and Ari split up the contents of the boxes among the various stations, Crystal began divvying up utensils, cutting boards, and bowls. People arrived in a trickle. She recognized a few familiar faces. Abbey Whittaker, one of Pru's best friends, who worked at the spa. Cayla Black, Kennedy's wedding planner. Essie Vaughn, Xander's dispatcher and office admin at the Sheriff's Department. Kennedy's boss, Denver Hershal, who owned Elvira's Tavern, and his girlfriend Misty something-or-other. There were other locals, whose names she didn't remember, and several other people she didn't recognize. Excited chatter filled the spaces. Athena couldn't help but wonder whether the students were really here for the food or to get a gander at her, the failed chef. Which one of them would ask her about the video or want to talk about the lost star?

Anxiety settled heavy in her gut, like a gravy spoiled by too much starch. Maybe this hadn't been such a good idea.

Logan pressed a hand to the small of her back and leaned in to whisper, "You just have to get through the first one right this second."

Right. And if she kept them busy, maybe no one would have time to ask her awkward questions.

Straightening her shoulders, Athena reminded herself that, for the next few hours at least, this was her kitchen. Her kingdom. She called the shots.

Clapping her hands, she stepped away from Logan. "Welcome, everybody. I'm Chef Athena

Reynolds. Today we're making maple-braised pork chops, with crispy Brussels sprouts, and creamed spinach. We'll be operating two and three to a station, so please grab an apron from my sous chef Ari, here, find your partner or partners, pick your spot, and we'll get started."

Everybody leapt into motion. It was mild chaos as people bumped into one another, paused to greet each other, and took their sweet time. Athena had to remind herself that they weren't trained, so she couldn't expect the efficiency of her staff at Olympus. Once everyone was settled at their respective stations, Athena took her position.

"Before we begin, I want to introduce you to the people who are making all this happen." She gestured to Crystal. "This is Crystal Blue. This diner is her place, and she's graciously offered up the space for our classes. It's also worth noting that she makes the best damned fried chicken I have ever eaten. If you're in town long enough, I encourage you to pop back by during regular business hours and get some."

Athena wasn't sure if she'd ever seen Crystal blush that much in all the years she'd known her.

"Oh now. Thank you. It was my grandmama's recipe."

"Family recipes are often the best. But food is only as good as the ingredients you put into it, and that brings me to my last introduction. Our ingredients today have all been provided by Logan Maxwell. Logan, do you want to tell these folks a little bit about what it is you do?"

He hesitated a few beats, clearly surprised at being put on the spot.

Athena arched a brow. *Turnabout is fair play, Farmer Boy.*

Evidently resigning himself, he straightened from the wall and joined her in the center of the room. "Well, to put it simply, I'm a farmer. But that really undersells the reality of what we do out at Maxwell Organics." He launched into his explanation, easy and in his element, clearly discussing his passion. The low cadence of his voice settled more of Athena's nerves, such that by the time he finished, she felt far more in control.

"In short, we're all about sustainable, organic agriculture."

A hand shot up. One of the out-of-towners. "Do you give tours of the farm?"

"Sure. From time to time. I think it's important for people to see where their food actually comes from."

"What about the farmer's market here in town?" This came from Abbey.

"We absolutely have a stand at the farmer's market during the season, and we sell CSA shares by the season. I'll be happy to provide a schedule at the end of class for those of you who are interested."

Athena stepped back into the center of the room. "Thank you, Logan. Now, let's get started. You'll notice that each station is fitted out with a hot plate, two cutting boards, knives, assorted bowls and ingredients. The pork is still in the refrigerator, brining until we need it later. This is everything we need to make the creamed spinach and the Brussels sprouts. It's good practice to pull out and organize every single ingredient before you begin so you don't run into any surprises by finding out when you're already in the middle of something that you're out of a key component. In French cooking, we call this *mise en place* or everything in its place."

Another hand shot up. Another of the out-of-towners.

Athena tensed and began rehearsing the carefully prepared rebuffs she'd worked out earlier this week. "Yes?"

"Is it true you studied with Francis Cano?" She said his name with the reverence the great chef deserved.

"I did." Her apprenticeship was something she certainly didn't mind talking about.

"What was he like?"

"Soft-spoken, brilliant, and utterly terrifying. He says things once and only once. If you miss it, he'll toss you out of his kitchen. But his food is so good it could start—or end—wars."

The woman grinned. "That is so cool."

Athena found a hint of a smile herself. "Yes, yes it was. Now, to begin, I'm going to get y'all to dice the onion. I'm sure everybody has their way to do this, but I'm going to show you the proper technique." She took them through it, demonstrating the correct way to hold the knife and walking them through the steps to create a nice, even dice without risking fingers.

She answered more questions as they went through the recipe. But no one asked about the video. No one said a word about Olympus or the lost star. As the class progressed, Athena realized that maybe her perspective on this whole thing was skewed. She'd become so accustomed to thinking of her restaurant and her life—which really had been one and the same for years now—as the center of the world. Any drama that impacted those things felt like big news that everyone knew because everyone in her circle was part of that same small, foodie world.

But these people seemed to know nothing of

all that. They knew the stuff that had been in her website bio. The big stuff that was readily out there in the non-trade publications. But the industry gossip, the details of her humiliation hadn't even pinged their radars. Because, surprise surprise, she wasn't the center of everything.

On some level she'd known that. But she'd needed this very real-world example to prove what Logan, Sean, and the rest of her family had been telling her for weeks. She wasn't ruined. Not to everyone.

For the first time since she'd walked out of Olympus, Athena felt like she could breathe. More, she felt the familiar spark of excitement at sharing good food with people. By the time the class sat down hours later, family-style, to eat the fruits of their labor, she was actually having *fun.*

"What are we cooking next week?" Essie asked.

"I'm not sure yet. Our menu today was inspired by what was freshest on the farm when we walked the fields this morning." With a quick look at Logan that was part question, part apology, Athena asked, "How would y'all like to come out to the farm before class starts next week? Get that tour and pick your own produce?"

The idea got an enthusiastic yes. Over the rest of the meal, they hashed out the details and Athena was already considering possible lessons.

Sunset streaked over the sky above the Ridge by the time the last student walked out of the diner.

Logan twisted the lock. "Well, I'd say that went pretty damned well."

More than a little giddy with relief, Athena began shoving tables back into their proper places. "It went far better than I expected."

"I enjoyed seeing you in your element. I always enjoy watching you cook." He glanced at the closed door to the kitchen, where Crystal was loading the industrial dishwasher, and lowered his voice. "Though I confess, I prefer watching you do it in nothing but my shirt."

"Well, you did promise to seduce me as a reward for getting through the class."

He hooked her around the waist and pulled her in. "Baby, you did so much more than just getting through. And maybe it's a stupid thing to say, since you're a badass chef and all, but I'm proud of what you did here today."

She'd received praise and accolades from some of the biggest names in the industry. But none of them gave her quite the same feeling as his quietly spoken words. "Thanks."

"So tonight, I say we celebrate. It happens, I've got a bottle of champagne chilled in my fridge and the season's first fresh strawberries. I expect you've got some ideas on how best to utilize those ingredients."

The hum in her blood that had stayed with her all through class flashed to a sizzle. Lips curving, she slid a hand up his chest and into the hair at his nape. "I expect I do."

"There's one thing, though." His expression hit somewhere between teasing and serious.

"What's that?"

"I might need all night to properly reward you. The class was that good."

"You want me to stay the night?"

"Not if you're not ready. But yeah, I want you to stay the night. I want to wake up next to you in the morning."

Athena's heart gave a hard knock against her ribs. All night with him. It sounded like heaven.

Rising up to her toes, she brushed her lips to his. "I like the way you think, Farmer Boy."

LOGAN JERKED at the first strident call from his feathered alarm clock.

Beside him, Athena jolted and curled tighter into her pillow as she spewed a string of vicious curses. "I'm going to wring that bastard rooster's neck and turn him into jerky."

Even as he wished he could wrap around her and find a better way to greet the day, Rudy crowed again. Logan pressed a kiss to Athena's shoulder. "Try to go back to sleep. No reason for you to get up this early while I see to the animals."

As soon as he vacated the bed, she confiscated his pillow and jammed it on top of her head. The sight of her in the thin, wispy light of dawn had him smiling. Leaving her there was maybe not quite what he wanted for a start to his morning, but a damned fine thing to wake up to nonetheless. Dragging on jeans and a t-shirt from the clean hamper, he unearthed some socks and headed downstairs to start his day.

The dogs rose from their beds in the den and padded over, wagging, butting his legs, his hands. He offered rubs and scratches and opened the door. Bo and Peep streaked off the porch and headed around the back of the house to do their business. Logan retreated inside to pour his first cup of coffee—brewed on a timer.

Thank God for modern technology. With the warm mug in his hands, he stepped out on the porch to survey his domain. Sunrise lightened the horizon, limning the fields and outbuildings in an ethereal light. He loved this time of day, loved the quiet before everything got up and running. For these first, few, quiet minutes, he enjoyed the peace and bone-deep happiness of knowing he was where he was supposed to be doing exactly what he was supposed to do. And today, he had a beautiful woman in his bed. One he'd spent his whole night making love to. The crash of no sleep would hit him later, but that was why God made coffee. Finishing his, he left the mug inside and began his chores.

There were animals to be fed, cows to be milked. By the time the milking system in the dairy barn was sanitized, his two high school interns—both members of Future Farmers of America—had arrived. They took over the milking process, so Logan headed out to deal with the pastured chickens. On the way, he nodded a wordless greeting to Sebastian, who was already out in the paddock working with Gingersnap, one of the rescues. The horse had put on weight in the past weeks. She still had a long way to go, but she already looked like a different animal.

Out in the west pasture, he released the chickens from their mobile coops. They spilled out, cackling and dancing with freedom before settling in to peck up bugs and grass and clover. Cleaning beneath the roosts, checking nesting boxes, and refilling water was rote for him. As was moving their mobile coops about a hundred feet so they'd have a new patch of grass and clover to roam and fertilize.

By the time Logan had worked his way through the rest of the list, he was thinking about another cup of coffee. He scrubbed up, wondering whether he could slip back into bed with Athena to give her a wakeup call that would make up for the rooster. Pleased with the idea, he toed off his boots on the porch and went back inside.

She was in his kitchen, wearing one of his

shirts. Her long legs were bare and her hair was still mussed from sleep and his hands as she moved with that graceful efficiency to make some kind of breakfast. It was exactly the image he'd had in his head. But this was better because her lips were curved in a quiet smile and the dogs were sprawled out at her feet, gazing up in adoration. She looked relaxed and happy. Logan knew what a big deal that was. That she was relaxed here, in this kitchen, on this farm. He understood what this place was to her. She just looked *right* here. In his kitchen, on his farm, in his life.

Drawn by the pretty picture she made, he stepped into the room. Athena looked up and offered him a sleepy, satisfied smile. It struck him in the chest, a mule kick to the heart that stole his breath.

He was in love with her. Completely, head over heels, totally gone, no turning back, in love with her.

"Hey. I found the coffee. You want more?"

Crossing the space between them in three

strides, he took her mouth, both because he couldn't *not* kiss her in that moment and to stop himself from saying anything foolish like, "I love you. Marry me and make this your home again." It didn't feel foolish in the least, but it was way the hell too soon for declarations. He wasn't about to do anything to send her running.

Breathless, she pressed her brow to his. "Well, good morning to you, too."

"You didn't have to get up."

"I hate your rooster. But my body actually does remember farm life. Once you were out of bed, I couldn't go back to sleep, so I thought I'd make you breakfast."

"And what is breakfast?"

"A bacon, white cheddar, and green onion frittata." She patted his chest. "Sit, have another cup of coffee, while I get this put together and in the oven."

He poured the coffee and kicked back against the opposite counter while she worked.

"I've been giving some thought to what we might cook for class next week."

She began to chatter on about recipe ideas. As long as he'd known her, she'd been passionate about food, but he'd never seen her this *excited*.

"Why are you smiling?" she demanded.

"It's just, I've never heard you quite like this before. Like your brain is firing at ninety miles an hour."

She paused, the cast iron skillet in one hand. "I feel...inspired. Like a weight that's been hanging on me for months is finally just...gone. I'm excited about food again, and I can't even begin to tell you what a gift that is." Sliding the skillet into the oven, she straightened. "And it's all because of you."

He'd wanted to be good for her, but he only just now realized how good she was for him, too. Her words were confirmation that she felt it too, this sense that they brought out the best in each other. She wasn't ready to see a future yet, wasn't ready to acknowledge the depth and breadth of what was between them. But this was a helluva start.

As that all fell into the category of things that might scare her off, he said only, "We make a good team."

"You're very, very good for me, Farmer Boy."

To stop himself from giving in and saying it anyway, he snagged her around the waist, drew her in. "I intend to be very, very good *to* you again." He ran a hand up her thigh and discovered she wasn't wearing any underwear beneath his shirt. "How long will that frittata take?"

Those smoky gray eyes went dark. "Long enough."

He lifted her onto the counter. "We'll just stay down here so you can keep an eye on things."

"Here?" She squeaked.

"Here."

By the time the frittata was ready, the rooster was no longer the loudest cry of the morning.

CHAPTER 11

$\mathcal{A}$s she paced in front of her last class, Athena was surprised at the pang she felt. Many of these people had come to every single class. She'd seen them learn and grow and embrace the joy of food, and that was a bigger high than she'd expected. It had been a long time since cooking had been entirely about the food. But while the whole thing had gone better than she'd anticipated, her relief that it was almost over outweighed the pang.

"Over the past few weeks, we've talked about how all cooking is really, at the root, about the interplay between fat, salt, heat, and acid. We've discussed how to choose the freshest produce, the best cuts of meat. You've practiced your knife skills. You've addressed the challenges of substitutions when you've got limited availability of ingredients. In each class, you've expanded your palate and focused on the food—no distractions—learning to appreciate the taste and quality of your component ingredients and how they interact to create a sum that's greater than their parts. As a chef, that's my favorite part of cooking." It had been good to be reminded that there was joy in addition to the control she craved.

There were a couple of new faces today, and she tried to incorporate them into the group that had already established its bonds. Smiling at the slim man with the finely-trimmed goatee who'd come up from Nashville for the class, she continued, "Now, I'm classically trained. I could teach you about master sauces or other fancy pants chef stuff. But the fact is, I'm not just a chef. I'm a Tennessee girl. A farmer's daughter.

I believe good food should be accessible." This whole farm-to-table series had been a great reminder of that. "I want to send you home today armed with recipes that you're comfortable recreating in your own kitchens. Recipes that you can head on down to Garden of Eden or out to Maxwell Organics to pick up and fix for supper without a whole lot of fanfare and fuss. I'm talking readily available, local ingredients that we're going to elevate to perfection."

"Bring it." Denver rolled his shoulders, flexing his big, tattooed arms as if ready to enter the boxing ring. "What are we making?"

"Oh, you're gonna like this," Athena promised. "As the centerpiece to the meal, we're making everybody's date night favorite: steak. I'll be teaching you about a variety of lagniappes—those little something extras that make a steak not to be missed. Alongside it we'll have potatoes boulangère and green bean bundles with a brown sugar balsamic reduction. For dessert, my take on a rustic, stone fruit tart. Let's get started."

"Was this the kind of thing you served at Olympus?"

The question caught Athena off-guard. Her heart skipped a beat, then leapt into a nervous tattoo. When had she stopped expecting questions about Olympus? Blinking at the guy from Nashville, she tried to formulate a proper response. What was his name again? Nelson something? "No. Olympus was far more focused on haute cuisine that was a blend of French, Greek, and Southern inspirations."

"So why not teach that?"

"Eden's Ridge isn't Chicago. We don't have access to the same wealth of ingredients here. And even if we did, that style of cooking falls well outside the scope of what can be covered in a class like this. The intent of these classes is to pass on practical skills that can be used to elevate food that you'll actually cook. Nobody goes home after a long day at work and makes escargots à la bordelaise. Not even me." Athena forced a smile and hoped it didn't look like a grimace.

She waited a moment to see if he'd pursue the line of questioning, but he merely nodded as if he were giving permission for her to carry on. The gesture rubbed her the wrong way and left her paranoid all through the lesson on making fresh pastry for the tart. He was polite, attentive, and followed instructions to the letter. Everything about him suggested he was a good student. But something about him kept her hackles raised.

The potatoes boulangère lesson went off without a hitch. The only questions were related to the dish itself. By the time the green bean bundles were wrapped and ready to go into the oven with the potatoes, Athena had almost convinced herself she was imagining the judgy stare from Nelson.

"Be sure to leave your bacon grease in the pan. It's going to become part of your balsamic glaze. Does everyone have your brown sugar measured out?"

"Was this the kind of stuff you cooked growing up?" Nelson asked.

Athena couldn't find anything actually wrong with the question but, again, there was something in his tone that didn't hit her right. "Some of it. I liked to experiment with the basic ingredients we had. Most of it we grew ourselves, so I was blessed with the experience of picking the components for dinner straight from the garden or gathering eggs fresh from the nest. As an adult, my palate has expanded considerably, but I still take great pleasure in simple ingredients." She intended her answer as a defense but realized it was true. Her return to Eden's Ridge had been very much about getting back to the basics. Filing that away as something to think about later, she went back to walking the class through the reduction.

There were a few mishaps during the rest of the lesson. Essie lost track of the sautéed mushrooms while talking with Cayla about a wedding she was planning. Abbey nicked a finger removing the pits from the plums they were using in the tarts. And Ford McIntosh, owner of Temptation Vineyards, was highly skeptical of cooking a steak any other way but on a proper grill. Athena was grateful for the bumps, as they kept her occupied and away from Nelson. She didn't like the guy. Didn't like the sense that he'd done a thorough Google search on her before joining the class. She'd resisted the urge to do that since she left Olympus, but his curiosity made her itch to check, to see what was out there and whether the furor had faded.

She wished Logan were here to talk her down. Hell, even his silent presence made her feel more steady and stable. He was so...unflappable. But he was tied up at the farm, helping Sebastian with repairs to the stable. She'd be headed out there as soon as class was over.

"Who's ready for dessert?" Crystal announced.

A resounding cheer went up in the dining room. Plates were cleared and her students paraded into the diner kitchen to carefully retrieve their respective tarts from the oven. Everybody set theirs on a trivet at the edge of their station and waited for Athena to inspect them.

"This is just like *The Great British Bake Off*," Ari giggled.

Relaxing, Athena quirked her mouth. "Should I do my best impression of Paul Hollywood, while you inspect for soggy bottoms?"

"I'd pay money to see that," Abbey said.

"We *did* pay money," Misty pointed out. "Do it!"

Laughing, they did a taste test of the tarts, declaring Essie's the hands down winner, with Denver and Misty's coming in a close second. Nelson seemed offended by the results, but by that point, Athena didn't much care. Class was essentially over and he'd be taking his sour ass back to Nashville, never to be heard from again. Hopefully.

As the leftovers were divvied up and packaged, Misty asked, "When is the next series and what's it going to be on?"

"Oh, uh..." Athena scrambled to think. Objectively, she had to consider the cooking school experiment a success. Her students had learned stuff. They wanted more. She'd made a little money that helped make up for the loss of normal income. And though it was an apples and oranges comparison, cooking in a group like this, being at the center of the camaraderie that had developed gave her the same spark of pleasure she'd felt cooking with her staff at Olympus. Good food prepared and appreciated by good people.

But she hadn't given any thought to more. She wasn't cut out to teach like this. Not all the time. There was way too much peopling, way too many details involved, way too much having to watch what she said and curb her perfectionist streak to accommodate their mostly novice skillsets. Doing that with Ari was one thing. Doing it on a scale this big? Hell no. But maybe once in a while she could tolerate it again. For special occasions.

"I'll have to give that some thought, but if you're definitely interested, please contact Celeste Keeling at the chamber of commerce to let her know. She'll send out an email or something whenever something else is planned."

"Great!"

"Can't wait!"

"This was awesome!"

"Everybody huddle up for a group selfie!" This came from Essie. Ari did the honors for that.

Somewhere in the middle, Nelson left without a goodbye. Good riddance.

Everybody gave a big round of applause and thanks to Crystal for donating her diner for the classes. Another to Ari for being sous chef extraordinaire. And finally a resounding one for Athena that left her feeling almost warm and fuzzy. Not that she'd admit it or risk losing her tough-as-nails reputation.

Logan had been right. He deserved a big reward for having this idea. For caring enough to believe that she could do this, to see that it was something that would be good for her, something she needed, even though she never would have thought of it herself. And then he'd gone and practically made it happen. All she'd had to do was get over herself and let it. Wasn't that how their entire relationship had gone? Him knowing her, seeing her, giving her just what she needed?

Damn, all this time at home was turning her into a sap. That was probably because of all the time she'd been spending with Ari.

Sure, it's all Ari.

The girl in question crossed her arms with a smirk. "You look like you're thinking about asparagus again."

Athena gave her a playful shove against the shoulder. "Go load the dishwasher, squirt."

LOGAN HAD HEARD rumors about the level of competition at a Reynolds family game night, but he'd never been a part of it before. Friendly insults and teasing were lobbed fast and furious across the big, farmhouse table. Kennedy and Xander sat across from him, Ari presided at the head of the table, and Athena leaned against him, currently trailing a finger up his thigh.

Logan laid a hand over hers, trapping it from going any further and draining sufficient blood from his head to handicap him. "What Texas blues-rock band, known for their beards and fur-lined guitars, made the 2004 list of Hall of Famers?"

As he finished the question, he shot a warning glance at his woman. She only smirked in response and tipped her head against his shoulder. She wasn't treating him as a fling or a secret. They hadn't talked about making any kind of formal announcement that they were together. But that easy affection, the open claiming of him in front of her family, gave Logan hope that this was truly the beginning of something lasting.

"Who is ZZ Top?" Kennedy announced.

"This is Trivial Pursuit, not Jeopardy. Answers should not come in the form of a question," Athena protested.

"I got it right, didn't I?" Kennedy looked to her husband for confirmation.

Xander nodded. "You did."

"Fine. Fine." Athena grabbed up the die and rolled, moving her token two spaces over to land on yellow. "Lay it on me."

Kennedy drew a card. "Which mathematical symbol, whose value is 3.14159, is celebrated with sweet desserts every March 14th."

"Duh. Pi Day."

"You are correct. That was totally a gimme question."

"You're the one who read it." Athena added a yellow wedge to her token. "Okay Pipsqueak, you're up."

Ari thumbed at her phone. "Mom and Dad say they may be late."

"Good for them. They deserve a proper date night. Once the baby comes, that'll be a lot harder," Kennedy said.

"You wanna bet they've gone and found somewhere to neck?" Athena asked.

"If Mom can pull that off seven months pregnant, I say more power to her."

Xander choked on his beer. "I did not need that mental image."

Ari rolled her eyes as she moved to a blue space. "You're such a guy, Xander. Okay, lay it on me."

As Athena pulled a question card, Ari's phone dinged again. She picked it up.

"Which state, famous for its gooey mud pies, is the birthplace of author John Grisham and media personality Oprah Winfrey?"

Ari frowned, clicking and swiping at the screen.

"C'mon now. No cheating by googling!"

An instant before Athena snatched the phone from her niece's hand, Logan caught the flash of distress. As Athena looked down at the screen, her own teasing smile faded, her cheeks turning ashen.

"What is this?" The eyes she lifted to Ari's were hard.

"I...it's a Google alert." Ari's chin wobbled.

"Why?" Athena's voice was soft, but there was the ring of steel beneath it.

Everything about the girl shrank as she closed in on herself. "I've been monitoring what people are saying about you."

Logan gripped Athena's thigh in warning as he felt her tense and coil with rage. Across the table, Kennedy scooted over and wrapped an arm around Ari's shoulders.

Athena swiped open the article. "That slimy bastard."

"What is it? What's wrong?" Kennedy asked.

Athena didn't answer immediately. Her face went grimmer and grimmer as she read, lines carving deep around her mouth. "I knew there was something off with him, with his questions."

Logan squeezed her leg again, reminding her they were there. "What is going on?"

She sucked in a breath and read, "'Athena's Fall From Olympus: The Unmaking of a Culinary Goddess.' His name was Nigel, not Nelson. Nigel Hitchens. He's a food critic from

Chicago, and he went undercover in my cooking class because he wondered what I'd been up to since I disappeared from the foodie scene in Chicago—oh because it's rumored I knew Michelin was yanking the star from Olympus and manufactured that whole outburst with Jayson to give everyone something else to talk about. He has *opinions* about what I taught, none of them flattering. And now, having seen the small town I come from, he understands that I could never have withstood the rigors of big city life and hopes I'll be very happy back in my greasy spoon, serving others who share my limited palate."

Logan's own temper, usually mild, ignited. How could this son of a bitch say any of those things? She was brilliant in the kitchen. And so the hell what if she was cooking something other than the over-priced, under-portioned pretentious stuff that most everyday people hadn't ever even heard of? That didn't make her food any less amazing, didn't make *her* any less. The desire to *do* something hit him like a freight train and the knowledge that there was nothing *to* do left him feeling impotent and frustrated. He understood better now some of what lay beneath Athena's anger issues.

Xander broke the ensuing silence. "What an asshole."

Athena inhaled another ragged breath, then another. Her hands curled to fists on the table, the skin on her knuckles going white. Her shoulders shook. Logan wanted to wrap an arm around her, to draw her in, but he suspected that would make her explode. Or break.

"I'm sorry." Ari's voice was small, miserable.

"None of this is your fault, honey," Kennedy assured her.

That needed to come from Athena to matter. But she was too far gone, spiraling through the rage and pain that had been banked these past weeks. The sight of it, the knowledge of it, cut Logan deep. He hated to see her hurting, hated that he could do nothing to make it better. But he could do damage control and keep the impending explosion from hurting anyone else.

"We're going for a walk," Logan announced.

Athena lifted her head, eyes sharp as a blade. "What?"

"You need a minute. We're going for a walk." Maybe he could talk her down, use his clinical skills to de-escalate the situation. Except, no, he couldn't sound like that's what he was doing. She'd balk at that. He'd figure it out on the way. "C'mon."

Without a word, she slid off the bench and stalked toward the back door.

Logan cast one last glance at everybody. "We'll be back. It'll be okay." Then he followed.

By tacit agreement, they took the trail down toward Opal Springs. Neither of them would be swimming tonight, but it was far enough away for privacy. He didn't touch her on the walk, wasn't sure how she'd take it. And he was busy trying to figure out how he was going to handle this without coming across like the therapist he still was.

At the water's edge, she whirled on him. "That petty, pissant, jackass insulted me, insulted Crystal, insulted everybody in this town. And he has the fucking *nerve* to discuss *my life?*"

Conscious that voicing his own fury over the situation would only fuel hers, he kept his tone calm. "Do you want to scream? Here's as good a place as any."

She let out a growl and began to pace. "This is a disaster."

He had to cut off that line of thinking before she spiraled out of control. She needed a reality check. "It's not. It sucks and it's hurtful, but in the end, he doesn't matter."

She hissed out a breath. "How can you say that?"

"He's one man."

"That article is going to be read by my peers. By everybody in the foodie world in Chicago. It'll go beyond that because it's going to stir up the circus again and that's only just started to die down."

And damn the man for setting her back

when she'd only just really begun to get past the whole thing. "He's not going to ruin you. That's not in his power."

"He can turn public opinion. And that influences my prospects."

Her prospects? The only prospects any of this would influence were those that weren't here. Was she honestly still thinking of leaving? After everything between them?

No. He shut the thought down with brutal swiftness. This was just her knee-jerk response. She hadn't really thought it through. And yet that her instinctive reaction involved her leaving had him wondering if they weren't as stable as he'd thought. Putting a lid on his own panic, he strove to remind her that she was past all this.

"In the world you left. The world you admittedly despise. Why would you want to go back to that? Why would you give a shit about what people like him think? They don't understand you."

"Because I want redemption, damn it. I want

a chance to prove myself again." Her voice cracked, her shoulders slumped. This time it was the tears underneath the rage that spilled out, and Logan wanted to beat the critic all over again.

He drew her in, holding tight as she let go of the control she held so dear, dropped the mask, and let him see the pain.

Of course she wanted redemption. He could understand her need for that. Why it was still important to her. Maybe he should've seen this coming. No matter that part of her had wanted out to begin with, she'd been forced out of that world by someone else. Another person taking her control.

When she'd cried herself out and quieted, he pressed a kiss to her hair. "You will prove yourself. Your way. But not in Chicago. Because you've found things here that are more valuable than whatever you left behind."

She sniffed. "I don't want it to be about the money. But Logan, that's a financial reality for me. I have to find something that can support me, support my dad. The clock's ticking on that. And the more shit like this happens, the less likely I am to be able to do that."

The weight of that responsibility had to be staggering, yet her determination to do right by her father never wavered. Her steadfastness just made him love her more, but he hated the stress it added to an already difficult situation.

He brushed at her tears with his thumb. "You have no idea how much it kills me not to have all the answers. To not even have any more good suggestions. I want to be able to fix this for you, and I can't. But I have faith that if you just hang on, just wait things out, the right thing is going to work itself out."

"Faith has never been my strong suit."

"Then I've got enough for us both."

When she sighed, all the fight seemed to drain out of her. "That'll have to be enough for now." Brushing a kiss against his cheek, she stepped away, already pulling herself back together. "We should get back. I need to apologize to Ari."

Taking her hand, Logan let her lead him back up the trail to the house.

He felt hollowed out from the whole exchange and a helluva lot less confident of where they stood than he had a half hour ago. He wanted to wrap her up and take her home so he could comfort them both, make love to her until she remembered all the reasons why staying was the only acceptable option. But, like everything else, it looked like that would have to wait.

CHAPTER 12

*I*n the wake of Nigel Hitchens' article, Athena kept a low profile, spending most of her time at the inn or the farm. She kept expecting somebody else to pop out of the woodwork to interrupt her life, set her back again. Though, she'd ultimately handled the whole critic situation with more resilience than she'd have managed without Logan to lean on. He'd been right. She didn't really want to be a part of the haute cuisine world anymore. She hated the needless pretension and the automatic assumption of classism that went along with it. Cooking for real people, normal people had given her more pleasure than she'd expected. Since she'd taken over the breakfast service at the inn, it had become something of a personal challenge to elevate humble ingredients to something more, something memorable. The end result had delighted guests and generated some good reviews for the inn. She'd contributed little enough to the family business since they'd started it last year, so it felt good to manage that much.

And yet that little voice calling her a failure, a nobody, still lingered in the back of her mind. She'd meant every word of what she'd said to Logan that night. That desperate desire for redemption ate up huge chunks of her days and dark hours of the night. She loved that he had faith that she'd figure out how to do that without capitulating and playing the game she'd been navigating for more years than she wanted to remember. She just wished she had that kind of confidence in herself.

"How's that béchamel coming, kiddo?"

"Nearly done," Ari reported.

Athena peered over her shoulder and made a few mental estimations on how much time she had, then began filling the crepes for their last guest of the morning. Some fresh bacon from the farm, crisped and crumbled with a nice melty brie and some apricot preserves. She folded and plated the crepes and held them out for Ari to ladle sauce over.

"Just a touch more than a drizzle. We don't want to drown them. Good. Now toss on some of those scallions you chopped earlier."

"These smell awesome."

"I'll plate up some for us while you take these out to our guest. Once we're done cleaning up, I'll take you on out to the farm."

"Awesome!" Ari slipped off her apron and scooped up the plate, taking it through the swinging door and on into the dining room.

Athena made up a second set of crepes for each of them, finishing the dishes off with Ari's béchamel—it was a damned fine effort—then perching on one of the barstools at the counter to cut in. She closed her eyes, savoring each distinct flavor on her tongue. The sweet of the preserves perfectly balanced the salt from the bacon, and the whole thing was mellowed out by the brie. The subtle afternotes of scallion and creamy béchamel were just enough to leave a hint of interest that made her want more. This. This was lovely. Simple and unexpected. She'd have to add this one to the recipe development file she'd started.

Ari hadn't come back by the time she finished her crepe. Athena figured she was either chatting up the guest, as she often did being the consummate innkeepers' daughter, or she'd headed upstairs to change. Popping the remaining crepe into the oven on warm, she began the cleanup. Some people hated dishes. Certainly, she'd been through a stretch where she had. But washing up, putting things to rights, had become its own form of moving meditation. At least so long as it wasn't in the middle of service. It was mindless and easy and gave her time to think.

No matter what horrible stuff had driven her back to Tennessee, had kept her here, Athena couldn't regret it. Logan had been right about that, too. She had found something more valuable than what she'd left behind. She'd found her love of food again. Reconnected with the joy of cooking. And in all truth, she couldn't have done that anywhere else. She had a feeling Logan was very much at the center of that. He was another of those valuable things she'd found. Alone in the kitchen, she could admit to herself that her reluctance to put herself out there, to figure out the next big thing, was as much to do with him as with fear of having her fall from grace in the foodie community confirmed.

Ari swung back through the door.

"Your crepe is in the oven."

The girl's hands were knit together and she wouldn't quite meet Athena's eyes.

"What is it?"

"The guest would like to talk to you."

Athena tensed but kept her tone even. "Is there a problem with the food?"

The big, dark eyes darted up, hopeful. "I don't think so. He's really excited." Then her gaze skittered away again.

Cursing herself for giving Ari any reason to worry about backlash from her, Athena squeezed her shoulder. "I'll go see what he wants."

She left her apron on, most comfortable with at least some of the armor of her trade. And it was armor. She strode into the dining room braced for battle, wondering who'd snuck into her quiet world now.

"I'm Chef Reynolds. You wanted to see me?"

The guy was all smiles, white teeth flashing in a tanned, curiously unlined face, though she pegged his age as older than he actually looked. Botox probably. Or maybe a face lift. He had California written all over him. That didn't put her at ease.

Mr. California held out a hand. "I'm Brock

Archer. I just had to meet the chef behind these fantastic crepes."

Accepting his enthusiastic handshake, she relaxed just a fraction. "I'm glad you enjoyed them, Mr. Archer."

"Sit for a minute. And please, call me Brock."

She didn't want to sit. She wanted to go back to her kitchen, but no matter what kind of a douchecanoe Jayson had been, he hadn't been wrong about being nice to the customers. So she slid into the chair across from him.

Brock beamed. "I ate at Olympus the year it opened. Absolutely life-altering. You are a seriously talented woman, Chef Reynolds. I was delighted to find out you were still here."

Her back went up again. What was she supposed to say to that? Apparently nothing because he leaned back in his chair and continued.

"I'm just gonna be a little nosy and ask: What is it you plan to do next? Are you opening a restaurant here? Will your family be expanding the inn?"

Ah, here was the trap. Was he a critic? He didn't have the vibe and seemed far too full of praise to fit that mold. So what was his angle? Realizing she had to give some kind of response, she hedged, "I'm still evaluating my options."

"Excellent! Then let me offer you another one. I've already been on the phone with my colleagues in L.A. and they're completely on board."

"On board with what?"

"We want to offer you a show."

Athena blinked, sure she hadn't heard him right. "Excuse me?"

"We want to put you on SizzleTV."

SizzleTV. One of the big competitors to the *Food Network* and Cooking Channel. Their hallmark was cooking competitions, showing the best of the best sweating it out, Thunderdome-style.

"As a competitor?"

"No—although that could be absolutely awesome and would be a good way to introduce you—" He whipped out his phone and typed something into it. "No, we want to offer you your own show."

"My own show," she repeated. Was she being punked? Was there a camera crew out in the hall waiting for the *Gotcha!* moment?

"Yes! We think you'd be fabulous. We want you to fly out to L.A.—our expense—to shoot a pilot episode. If the powers that be like it—and we have no doubt that they will—you will be the next SizzleTV star."

Athena's brain felt like congealed polenta. "I'm sorry, I know I'm a little slow here, but... you want to put me on TV?"

"We do." He rambled on about timing and production schedules and a lot of details Athena didn't catch.

She'd never even considered television. In truth, she had no idea whether she'd be any good at it. She wasn't what anyone could call congenial. But the idea of her own show, of something that could finally, truly focus on the food—food that would, hopefully, be stuff normal people would want to and be able to cook—that was exactly what she was looking for.

"What do you say?"

She'd wanted a new direction, some way to use her skills and earn back her reputation. Logan had said to think of something outside the box. This definitely fit the bill.

Mom, what was it you used to say? When one door closes, somebody opens a window?

Sucking in a breath, Athena offered Brock a tentative smile. "I guess I'm going to Los Angeles."

THE SIGHT of Athena's little car coming down the drive pulled Logan in from the fields. Bo and Peep streaked across the field in front of the ATV, black and white blurs through the green. They were already dancing around the front of the car as he parked by the house. Athena and Ari climbed out.

"Well, there are my two favorite girls." He sensed the tension between them before the words even made it out of his mouth. "Y'all want some tea or lemonade?" Maybe if he got them inside, he could get to the bottom of whatever that was and diffuse the situation.

Ari glanced from Athena to him, a frown tugging the corners of her mouth. "I'm gonna head on to the stable."

Well, all right then.

The taciturn routine wasn't like her. Worry draped over her like a wet blanket, squelching her usual bubbly nature. Did that mean there was something he needed to worry about too or was this some lingering awkwardness between her and Athena from the incident on game night?

If Athena registered Ari's mood, she gave no indication. Striding over, she rose to her tiptoes, pressing her mouth to his in a smacking kiss. "Hey, handsome. Got a little time? I want to talk to you about something."

With another glance at her niece's retreating back, he nodded. "I can make some."

Grateful for a break from the rising heat of the day, he led her back to the kitchen.

"Do I want to know what all that was about?"

Athena shrugged. "Moody teenager is moody."

"Did y'all have a falling out?"

"Not exactly. That's part of what I wanted to talk to you about. Let's get something to drink, and I'll tell you about it."

While he poured a couple glasses of lemonade, she grabbed dog biscuits from the jar on the counter—biscuits she'd baked herself—and put Bo and Peep through their paces. Sit. Stay. Shake. Lay down. Roll over. At the end of it, the pair of them gobbled up the biscuits and pressed against her legs in adoration.

"Okay, okay. I love y'all, too. Let me sit."

Curling into a chair at the table, she wrapped her hands around the glass, trailing one finger through the condensation. One leg bounced and her eyes fairly sparkled. Something was definitely up.

"Okay, spill it. What's going on?"

Her lips curved into a grin. "You said if I waited long enough, something would work itself out. You were right."

The smile invited him to join in the good news, but dread began to curl in his gut instead. He blanked his face, retreating to clinical distance for the discussion because he had a feeling he was gonna hate where this was going. "Oh?"

"This wasn't even on my radar as a possibility, but I got contacted by an exec with SizzleTV today. They want to give me my own cooking show."

It wasn't what he'd been expecting. He'd thought it would be maybe a job offer taking her to New York or Boston or some other big metropolis as head chef to…somewhere. But he wasn't sure this was any better. "A cooking show?"

He listened. Thanks to his clinical training

he was a hell of a good listener. But his mind spun with implications and questions as she told him what she knew, which, by his estimation, wasn't nearly enough.

"Anyway, I'm flying out to L.A. tomorrow. I'll be meeting with execs and filming the pilot episode." She all but vibrated with excitement, which made him feel like an asshole for bursting her bubble. But one of them had to be responsible here.

"Don't you think this is awfully fast? What do you know about this guy? This company?"

"The guy checks out. Maggie's heard of him. And I know SizzleTV is the biggest competition the *Food Network* has. A show with them would go a helluva long way to eradicating the damage from that video. This is my shot at redemption, Logan. At rebuilding my professional reputation. At being somebody again."

Who did she think she was now?

He shook his head. "I thought you'd made so much progress since you got home, but ever since that asshole critic was here, you've been reverting to old patterns. This is just more regression."

The excitement in her expression chilled and hardened. "Excuse me? Regression? Old patterns? *Progress?* Are you psychoanalyzing me, Logan?"

Was he? Damned straight. "Yeah. Because right now, you need it."

He'd promised himself he wouldn't do this with her, but he had to make her see reason. "If you go out there, if you do this show, it's just gonna be a whole other set of pretentious assholes. Except instead of food critics and the like, it'll be network execs and the money men and whoever the hell else who's going to end up telling you what to do and how to do it. You won't have control. It won't be about the food, and you'll hate it. Haven't you learned anything these past few months?"

"This is for my own good, right? Because I wouldn't know that, and never mind what I actually want, what I'm telling you I want." She stared at him with a mix of disgust and fear that curdled his gut.

But she couldn't mean what she was saying. She couldn't have thought it through because that meant she was okay with leaving Tennessee, leaving her family. Leaving him.

Panic made the wheels of his brain slow and stutter as he tried to figure out how to deescalate the situation.

"Have you been trying to head shrink me this whole time?" she demanded.

No sense in lying now. "It's part of my training. It's not like I turn it off like a light switch. It doesn't change anything." The moment he said it, he knew he'd fucked up. The energy in the room seemed to suck toward her, gathering for what he knew would be an explosion. But hell, he was in it now.

"Doesn't change anything?" The hiss of her voice was low and dangerous. "How can you say that? You've spent all this time watching and analyzing everything I say, everything I do and figuring out how to *handle* me." Her voice rose in volume with every word, until the dogs flinched. A momentary flash of contrition crossed her features as she reached out a hand to soothe them both.

"It's how I deal with everybody. It's called getting to know you and being respectful of who you are."

Her gray eyes went to slits. "Is that supposed to make this better?"

Yeah, he wasn't even gonna get into that. "You're veering off-topic here. We're talking about L.A. and why this isn't a good idea."

"There's not a 'we' here, Logan." Her words struck him like bullets. "You're the only one who doesn't think it's a good idea."

Ari clearly didn't think it was a good idea either, but he wasn't going to bring her into the discussion. "Because it's not going to make you happy." Couldn't she *see* that?

Athena crossed her arms, the picture of belligerence. "And you're the expert on that?"

What the hell did she think he'd been doing since she came back to Eden's Ridge? As his own temper rose, his grip on that careful impartiality began to slide. "I'd say I've done a pretty fucking good job of it up to now."

Her nostrils flared. "I don't have the luxury to make decisions purely around what makes me happy. I have a financial responsibility to take care of my father."

"Stop using your dad as an excuse and own up to how much of this is about soothing your damaged ego."

Her head kicked back as if he'd slapped her, but he couldn't stop now. He had to make her see.

"You've said over and over again how you want to prove yourself. But who the hell are you proving yourself to, Athena? What does the adulation of a bunch of total strangers actually get you? What the hell good is it when everything and everybody else you care about, who cares about you, is here?"

Feeling the shift again, he braced for the explosion. It came in the form of her hands slapping the table. Then she gripped it, hard enough her knuckles pressed white against the skin of those scarred, capable hands. "Everybody who cares about me understands that I *deserve* this chance." Her chair screeched across the wide-planked floors as she shoved up. "I was meant for bigger things than a small-town life. I'm not going to hold myself back because of fear—mine *or* yours."

She started to walk out and panic blasted through his anger like lightning. If she went out to California, he'd lose her.

"You'll hate it." His words had her hesitating at the threshold, so he spit out the rest of it, fueled by frustration and fear. "You'll hate it, and you'll blame them, blame circumstances, blame anybody else but yourself for making that choice. Make a different one, Athena."

He saw the barbs strike home in the way her spine snapped straight.

Sometimes the truth hurts. He hated to be the one to do it. But maybe now they could talk about this openly, honestly. Even if it was at top volume. He'd take a raging fight over nothing at all.

But Athena didn't turn. She didn't fire back with the fury he'd expected. Her words, when she spoke, were low and measured. "This is the only choice I've got."

Without another word she walked out of his kitchen and, he suspected, out of his life.

CHAPTER 13

"I don't know how you did this haul so often in the last year." Stepping into Maggie's apartment, Athena dumped her bag and stumbled over to collapse onto the sofa. "How is it that Tennessee feels like a million miles further from L.A. than Chicago does?"

"Well, having to drive hours to the airport in Nashville before even getting on the plane has a lot to do with it. I'm gonna guess by the fact that you're doing a fine impression of a throw blanket on my couch that you would vote for a nap before going out for dinner?"

Throwing an arm over her eyes, Athena considered just passing out right here and skipping food altogether. Then her stomach growled. "Please, God, don't make me people anymore. Can't we just get takeout?"

"Seriously? After months in Eden's Ridge, you're back in a city, with access to every kind of food known to man, and you'd rather stay in? What happened to you, girl? I've never known you to bail on the chance to try new cuisine."

"I'm just wiped out. I guess I've lost some tolerance to the volume of people in the city since I left Chicago. It's the longest stretch I've been home since I left at eighteen." How had she not realized that before? She'd expected to be itchy and dying to get the hell back out of Tennessee. Instead she'd slid back into the rhythm of it like a pair of favorite jeans.

"Well, if this whole show pans out, you'll

have plenty of time to try everything you want out here. And there's a lot."

Athena waited for the usual buzz of excitement that accompanied the idea of culinary exploration in a new place. But it didn't come. Maybe she was just too damned tired. She hadn't slept for shit last night, too anxious about the trip, about how this meeting with network executives would go. Too upset at the fight she'd had with Logan. She didn't know where they stood. Maybe that was the answer in and of itself. She hadn't wanted to get in too deep for exactly this reason. A show would mean she'd be moving to Los Angeles, at least for the bulk of the year. Maybe some people could maintain a long distance relationship from three thousand miles away. She wasn't one of them. And what did that matter, anyway? He wasn't the guy she'd thought he was.

"Who's not the guy you thought he was? Logan?"

Athena peeked out from her arm, startled to

realize she must've spoken aloud. Dammit. Maggie would never let it alone now. "Yeah."

"You're gonna have to explain that because every other conversation we've had you've been your version of giddy about him."

Insulted, Athena sat up. "I was not giddy."

"I said your version. And giddy was Ari's term."

Athena rolled her eyes. "Of course it was."

"What happened?"

He'd ruined her high, that's what happened. When she should've been able to bask in the excitement and thrill, instead she'd been sucker punched. Knowing her sister would just wait her out, Athena grabbed up one of the colorful pillows and wrapped her arms around it. "I went out to the farm yesterday to tell him about the show."

Maggie moved into her kitchen and opened a bottle of wine. "I gather that didn't go well."

Athena snorted. "That would be an understatement. This is the first legitimate offer I've had that could salvage my career, and he shot the idea right on down. After being so sup-portive of me this whole time, when push came to shove, he was just paying lip service." She accepted the glass of wine. "Thanks. And—*and*—not only was he absolutely against the idea of the show, he's been shrinking my damned head this whole time!"

Maggie folded herself onto the other end of the couch. "He what?"

"He's a therapist."

"I thought he was a farmer."

"He was a therapist, or almost, before he left the last semester of school to be a farmer."

"So he never practiced?"

"He's been practicing on me, apparently. Using his shrinky skills." Athena scowled, re-playing everything he'd ever said to her, won-dering what else she'd dismissed as casual conversation.

"Used them to what exactly? Coerce you? Manipulate you?" Maggie's expression re-mained neutral, but the steel in her tone said she'd castrate anyone who tried.

Athena wanted to say yes, but couldn't. Logan hadn't coerced or manipulated her. Not in any castration-worthy way. No matter how angry she was, she knew he wasn't a bad guy. It was just— "He acted all blasé about the whole thing, like he left the program, he's just a farmer, but the whole time he's taking in everything I say and do and analyzing me."

"To what end?"

She thought about what he'd said. "He said it was about getting to know me and being respectful of who I am."

"That doesn't sound so terrible."

"Then why does everything in me want to reject that?" Athena sipped at the wine, barely registering the bold notes of plum that underscored the grapes.

"You know why."

She did know why. He was just like those assholes who'd analyzed her without her knowledge or consent and used that to take her away from her father.

"But you're saying he didn't get to know you

and then use that against you?" Maggie asked into the protracted silence, like she wanted to be sure there was no valid opportunity to mete out violence.

Athena thought about it, and because she was messed up and tired, because Logan's reaction to her news and that whole conversation had really thrown her, she had to think really hard. But no, Logan hadn't betrayed her; he wasn't like the counselors in her past. But there was something. He'd done something, because she'd felt...*something*.

"Athena?"

"No, he didn't use it against me. The fact is, he does know me. So well it makes me feel..." She struggled to find the words to explain that feeling of exposure.

"Vulnerable?" Maggie suggested.

"Yes. And I hate that. I hate that so much."

"You always have. As long as I've known you. But I've never asked you why that is. What are you so afraid of?"

She'd had a big chunk of sleepless night and

hours on a plane to think about it. "Because it means he can hurt me." Setting her wine aside, Athena drew her knees up and rested her cheek against them. "I didn't mean to let him so close."

Maggie studied her over the rim of her glass. "It's not that he can hurt you. It's that he has."

"Yes," Athena whispered. "In the heat of things he said none of this was about my father. That it's just about my reputation and ego. I get that I have a titanic ego. It goes with the territory of my profession. But literally everything I have done in my career has been about attaining maximum success so that I could take care of Dad. I chose paths I wouldn't otherwise have chosen just because it would mean more commercial success."

You'll hate it. And you'll blame everyone but yourself for having made the choice.

On some level he'd been right, damn him. She had hated it. Not all of it, not all the time. But in the end, she had hated it. But he was wrong about the choice. She didn't have one. Not really.

Maggie sipped her wine, considered. "I think a lot of it has been about that, yeah. But you're a chef, not an accountant. If it was just about the money, you could've gone into a multitude of other more lucrative fields. You chose food because it's your passion. So there's a lot of you bound up in it, too. As there should be."

Athena bristled. "Are you siding with him?"

"I'm not taking sides here. I'm asking questions to clarify. Given your level of pissed off about this, I have to ask if he's right. If your dad wasn't part of the equation, would you still make the same decision to come out here, to try this?"

If she didn't have the financial burden of her father's care, if she didn't have a ticking time clock over her head, would she still choose the show? "After everything I've been through the past months? Yeah. Yeah, I would. Because I feel like a failure. A disgrace, and I want to reclaim my reputation. You, of all people, get that."

"Yeah, I do. It's why I'm way out here instead of home. Because here I can be something other than 'that girl who got knocked up in high school.'" Maggie tipped back the rest of her wine. "What did Logan say when you explained that?"

I was meant for bigger things than a small town life. I'm not going to hold myself back because of fear—mine or yours.

"I'm...not sure I did explain it. Not very well. The discussion kind of degenerated."

"I can only imagine. Well, you're here. You're going to go to that meeting tomorrow and wow the hell out of them. You'll see what there is to see about whether this opportunity is what you want it to be. And if it is, know that I will be ecstatic to have you here. I miss family. I miss home. It's hard being this far from everybody." She set her glass aside. "You know. It was the same for you in Chicago."

Yeah, it had been. She'd lived in big cities on her own since she left home at eighteen. Every single one had been an exciting new opportunity. A chance to learn something new. That had been enough to override the inherent homesickness. After a while, she'd forgotten what life had been like before. She'd learned to do without the tight bonds of community and the daily presence of her sisters. But she couldn't help but think that it would be so much harder now that she'd had a solid reminder of what home actually felt like.

And if it was Logan's arms and the farm she thought of rather than the inn where she'd spent her teen years, well, she'd learn how to do without them too.

"BROTHER, YOU LOOK LIKE SHIT." Xander accompanied that pronouncement by pushing past Logan into the house. Porter and Flynn trailed behind him.

"What the hell are y'all doing here?" But he knew.

Athena had left for L.A. this morning

without a word. Logan shouldn't have been surprised by that. She hadn't come out when he'd dropped Ari home yesterday, not even to pick up their fight. Maybe in her mind it was done. Maybe they were done.

And he didn't have anyone to blame for that but himself.

"I brought bourbon," Xander called from the kitchen.

Logan's beverage of choice for drowning regrets. Exactly how much had she said to her sisters before she left town?

His old friend had already retrieved glasses from the cabinet and poured two fingers into one. He offered it. "Here."

Logan eyed it for only a second before accepting the glass. He was done with work for the day. "What did she say?"

"Not a bleedin' thing," Flynn said. "She packed up and lit out this mornin' with barely a word. Not even to say she was excited about the prospect of a job."

"Our wives are convinced something's

wrong between the two of you, and given your reaction just now, I'm guessing they're right. What happened?" Xander demanded.

Logan took a hefty swallow of the bourbon, rolling it in his mouth a moment before swallowing down the fire. "I guess you could say we had our first fight."

Porter reached for the bottle and poured himself a smaller glass. "About this thing in California?"

"Yeah."

"Ari's pretty upset about it," Flynn said.

"Yeah, she was when they came out here yesterday. She doesn't want Athena to leave. Neither do I."

Xander kicked back against the counter and crossed his arms. "Did you say that?"

How would she have responded to that tactic? To an honest declaration. *Athena, I'm in love with you. Don't go.*

It hadn't even occurred to him to take that route, and now he wouldn't get the chance.

"No. I tried to be logical about the whole

thing. To point out why it wasn't the right choice for her." Logan tossed back the rest of the bourbon and winced. "That's what I meant to do."

"But not what you actually did?" Flynn prompted.

"I could have handled it better." Reaching for the bottle, he poured more bourbon. "I lost my temper and said some stuff I shouldn't." He'd hurt her, and that had never been his intention.

Xander studied him with that flat, cop stare. "I can count on one hand the number of times I've seen you lose your cool in all the years I've known you. What set you off?"

"She's not being rational about this. And she's not being honest with herself about what she wants. What she needs. She's throwing herself at this idea of a show full-force, still reaching for the same world, the same shit that made her miserable in the first place, using bullshit justifications that make it not really about her and her choices. I really thought she'd figured it out, that she'd changed."

The next shot of bourbon only seemed to inflame that rare temper he thought was banked. "But hell, people don't change. I know that. That's the biggest reason I got the fuck out of psychology. Because I knew I'd never be able to sit in session with people, week after week, year after year, and them not take responsibility for their role in their own shit."

Porter and Xander exchanged a look. "You didn't actually say that, did you?"

"Not those precise words but something to that effect." He wished he'd been calmer. Wished he'd been able to frame his thoughts some other way. Athena was a rebel. Tell her not to do a thing, and she'd go ahead and do it to spite everybody, including herself. He knew this about her, knew an ultimatum would go over like a lead balloon. And he'd done it anyway.

I won't be held back by fear. Mine or yours.

She hadn't been a hundred percent wrong.

Logan was afraid of losing her to her career. But he wasn't holding her back because of that. Was he?

"You're an idiot—speaking of people not learning to take responsibility for their role in their own shit. Didn't you learn anything from what happened with Maisey?" Xander demanded.

Of course he was gonna go there.

"Who's Maisey?" Flynn asked.

"Are you gonna tell this, or am I?" When Logan just growled, Xander continued. "Maisey Howell was his girlfriend in college and grad school. They were together for, what, three years? Started dating his senior year at UT. Stuck together when he stayed for grad school. She had some...what'd you call it? Adjustment problems, when she graduated and hit the real world."

Because Logan knew the specifics far better, he picked up the tale. "Graduating with honors in the middle of a recession and not being able to find a decent job did a number on her. Lot of frustration, lot of anxiety problems. She talked to me about it a lot. Of course she did. I was her boyfriend. But I was also a therapist in training, and the stuff she was saying, the dark place she was headed into, concerned me. Enough that I spoke to her parents, just to find out if they'd seen anything that worried them, too."

"That doesn't sound so unreasonable," Flynn said.

"Yeah, well, turns out she had a history of depressive episodes, so what I said, the things I shared about my own concerns, were giant red flags for them. They had her hospitalized for evaluation. It was only a week, and I thought, given where her head was, that it was a good move. But when she got out, she was livid. Convinced I'd totally broken her confidence. It had taken her all of college to get out from under her parents' thumbs, and what I'd done put her right back under the microscope. She didn't care that I'd done it out of love because I was worried about her. For her, that was it. She couldn't trust me anymore, and we were done."

He rolled the empty glass in his hand. "But that's not what happened with Athena."

"Isn't it?" Xander challenged. "You tried to use your clinical judgment on somebody you're in a relationship with. With good intentions, I'm sure, but you still did it. So maybe you're just like everybody else and aren't changing either. Because here's a thing: with Maisey, you didn't know all the history. You didn't know how her parents would react by taking away all her control. But this time, you knew the history. You knew Athena's experience with counselors resulted in them yanking her out of her home, and that she's been something of a control freak ever since."

"To put it mildly," Porter muttered.

Fuck me. Logan scowled. "So I'm a hypocrite?"

"I'd say you're human and in love with a prickly, stubborn woman who challenges you at every turn. One whose choices might be taking her far away from you." Flynn lifted his glass. "I'd say fucking up and saying the wrong thing under those circumstances is pretty under-standable."

"Maybe," Logan conceded.

Xander tipped the bottle against Logan's glass. "For the record, did she actually tell you what she thinks this is going to be?"

"Her shot at redemption. She was clear enough about that."

Xander and Flynn exchanged a knowing look.

Logan slapped his glass down on the counter. "What? What is it you know?"

"Well, it's just that she talked all this over with her sisters before she even came out here yesterday. They went through all of this," Flynn explained.

"She flat out said that even if it worked out, she didn't think she wanted to do this forever," Xander added. "But she wanted to give it a try, see what doors it might open. And if she does decide to walk away from it, she gets to do it on her own terms."

Logan closed his eyes as the full measure of

his screwup hit home. He'd accused her of pursuing all this out of sheer ego. But it hadn't been that simple. It hadn't been about keeping up appearances in her professional circles. It had been about going out on her own terms, when she had the final say, the ultimate control. *That* was her ego. That was what he should have understood when she came to him, because he knew her. But he'd let his own upset, his own panic at the idea of losing her get in the way. And now that he'd pissed her off, driven her away, he'd probably killed any chance of being in her "Stay" column after all was said and done.

"I am a dumbass," Logan announced.

Flynn raised his glass again. "It's a wise man can admit it."

"But I'm not completely wrong. Every instinct I've got says this show is a mistake. That it's not gonna be what she thinks it will be."

"Maybe it won't be. But it's on her to figure that out," Porter said.

Miserable, Logan eyed the last quarter of

the bottle. "I just wanted to protect her from more pain and disappointment."

"No matter how well-intentioned you are, she won't thank you for it. Athena's always been one who has to learn things the hard way. We've had to let her," Xander said.

"How the hell do you stand it? Watching somebody you care about walk into a mistake?"

"You accept that it's their mistake to make," Porter pronounced. "And you're around to help with the fallout. No judgment. No matter how much you have to swallow your tongue."

"And in the meantime, you drown your urge to act in your favorite form of spirits. More bourbon?" Flynn suggested.

CHAPTER 14

*I*n the backseat of the cab, Athena smoothed her sweaty palms over her skirt. She wished she'd gotten the chance to talk to Maggie again this morning. Her sister had been up and out early for work, leaving Athena to get ready for this meeting on her own. Conscious of meeting with a bunch of Hollywood types and the need to make a good impression, she'd spent a lot more time and effort on her appearance than usual. Hair. Makeup. A dress. Heels she hoped never to see again. Stuff she usually reserved for major events like weddings and funerals. She wished like hell she could do this in jeans and boots. But they were expecting a professional chef, not a farm girl.

Realizing she'd clenched her hands in her skirt, she relaxed them, smoothing the fabric again. Why the hell was she thinking about being a farm girl right now anyway? She wasn't a farm girl. Hadn't been since she was a kid. A couple of months hanging out with Logan didn't change that, no matter how comfortable she'd gotten back on the farm.

He hadn't texted or tried to call. Not to apologize and not to try to talk her out of this. That was fine. She didn't actually want to talk to him anyway. Except that she did. She ached to hear the sound of his voice soothing the nerves and telling her she'd get through this meeting. That she'd shine and impress. But that was the fantasy version of Logan.

The real one had made it perfectly clear he wouldn't tell her that. The real one was going to blame her for making this choice in the first place because it wasn't the one he wanted. He wanted the one that would keep her in Tennessee, support her dad, and be magically, professionally fulfilling for her. Because apparently the real Logan believed in unicorns.

And damn it, why was she thinking of him? Again. She didn't need all that in her head before this meeting. She needed to be on top of her game, focused on...whatever they were going to throw at her.

"Lady?"

She jolted at the sound of the cabbie's voice. "Yeah?"

"We're here."

Turning her head, she caught sight of a gleaming steel and glass building with a larger-than-life version of SizzleTV's logo front and center. "Oh. Sorry."

She dug out cash to pay the fare and stepped out of the car, muttering a silent prayer that she didn't take a header in these heels and embarrass herself. Inside the spacious, modern lobby she paused, searching for the reception desk.

"Athena!" Brock's voice boomed and he

strode over, his hand already outstretched to take hers and shake it. "I'm so glad you made it."

Years of Joan Reynolds' lessons in manners had her murmuring, "Thank you for having me."

Tucking her hand in his elbow, Brock towed her toward the elevator. "We've got just enough time for a tour of the studios before we meet with everybody."

He showed her production rooms and sets for shows she watched herself. She snapped a few pictures of those to text Ari. Her niece wasn't any happier with her than Logan, but maybe she'd at least think it was cool. By the time they made it into the network kitchens, she began to relax a little. The gleaming commercial grade ranges and ovens elicited a sharp stab of professional lust. She wished they could have their meeting in here, so she could cook and talk and distract from her awkwardness with food. But Brock was already dragging her away, down a hall and up an elevator to a floor of offices.

The conference room he hauled her into was a hive of activity. The sheer number of people overwhelmed her, so she missed the names of most of them during the introductions. Then they were seated, her at one end of the big conference table, and everybody was looking at her.

Athena fought not to fidget.

At the other end of the table, the guy whose name she didn't remember but who was clearly the One In Charge, kicked back in his chair. "We're so excited you're here."

Okay, deep breath. You've got this. You're a badass chef and you are in control. She had no idea how this meeting was meant to go, but her mother had always said start as you mean to continue. Straightening her shoulders, Athena did her best to channel Maggie's cool, calm, collected nature. "I appreciate the opportunity. Mr. Archer hasn't said anything just yet about the specifics of what y'all were thinking but I had a few ideas I'd like to share."

Money Man nodded. "Sure, we'd love to hear them."

This was what she'd used to distract herself when she couldn't sleep the past couple of nights. "You're in the food industry, so I know you're all familiar with the farm-to-table or farm-to-fork movement."

She caught nods and noises of agreement.

"It's something I've always felt very passionate about. Knowing where your food comes from, how it's grown or raised, and being able to make menus and meals from what's peaking at any given time. Food is—or should be—inherently seasonal. I was raised on a farm, so this is something I know better than many. And it's something I've been reconnecting with the past few months."

She had a flash of Logan in jeans and a t-shirt, hands covered in good, rich earth as he lifted the latest, gorgeous produce from his land. The land that had once been hers.

Shaking the image away, she continued. "Now certainly in the restaurant scene, farm-to-table isn't new. But it is trending, and less attention has been paid to it from the standpoint of cooking television. What I would really love to do is bring that reality to viewers. Highlight organic farmers around the country and really show people what you can do with seasonal organics and heirloom ingredients. I think it could fill a niche for your viewership that nobody else is really playing with."

Money Man steepled his fingers. "That's an interesting concept, but not quite what we had in mind."

She'd assumed they had other ideas, so she settled back in her chair to listen, channeling the polite mask she always used when dealing with restaurant patrons.

"As you may not know, SizzleTV was really founded on competition. We've expanded our programming options, certainly, but our bread and butter around here is cooking contests with lots of pop and personality."

Athena frowned. "Mr. Archer said you weren't looking at me as a contestant."

"He's correct. We're not. We definitely want you as a host, but we're looking for something with more punch, more drama."

"Drama?" A sick feeling set up in her gut.

"We're more interested in having you be the face of SizzleTV's answer to *Kitchen Nightmares.*"

A show that was all about going into other restaurant kitchens and tearing them apart before putting them back together to be a success. She understood the appeal of it. Had watched a lot of it herself. It was one of the things she and Ari had bonded over. But being entertained and being the entertainer were two very different things.

"You...don't want me to cook?"

Money Man waved a cheerful hand. "I'm sure you're a perfectly wonderful chef, but we want to capitalize on your existing notoriety. You were utterly magnificent in your rage and viewers will eat that up. A female Gordon Ramsay."

They'd seen the video. Of course they had.

People like this would do thorough internet research on any prospective host. Certainly her reputation would matter to public opinion, but…to do this, to keep her most embarrassing moment in the limelight…

Money Man was still talking, an avaricious gleam in his eyes as he discussed concepts and ratings and how the show would be structured, what their expectations of her really were. All centered around cementing her reputation as an unprofessional hothead.

Logan was right. It wasn't about the food. She wouldn't have control. And none of this was what she'd hoped it would be. This wasn't even the world of pretension she'd left. This was worse. They were asking her to debase herself for the sake of ratings. That wasn't a choice she could make. Not even for her father's sake. Apparently, she had a line, and this was it.

"I'm sorry. I wish Mr. Archer had been forthcoming about this from the beginning. I came out here under the impression you wanted me to do a cooking show. Something that would take advantage of my expertise as a chef. I have no interest in losing my temper on camera on a weekly basis."

Everybody started talking at once, a storm of words attempting to placate or convince. It all sounded like the buzz of so many bees, swarming around her, waiting to sting.

Embarrassed, humiliated, Athena shoved back from the table, needing to escape before she lost her shit right here. "I apologize for wasting everyone's time."

Before anyone could stop her, she marched out of the conference room, head held high. She made it to the elevator without being stopped, and as soon as the doors slid shut, she slipped off the hated heels.

She'd been a fool. Desperate and blind. And Logan, for all his head shrink talk, had been trying to save her from exactly this. Why hadn't she listened?

He knew her. Understood her. Did it really matter how? He saw *her.* And he didn't want to change her, didn't want her to be anyone other than who she was. He hadn't used his training in a bid to take her control away, in fact. He wanted success for her on *her* terms. She was an idiot to walk away from that.

Well, Farmer Boy, I'm listening now. And I'll take your search for unicorns over this any day.

The elevator doors opened to the lobby, and Athena took off running. She had to get back to Tennessee.

A VOLLEY of manic barking jerked Logan from sleep. He jackknifed up in bed, hands curling to fists to defend against…what? The dogs had already bolted from the room, the skitter of their paws against the wood of the stairs echoing in the otherwise quiet house before he registered the knocking.

What the hell?

Scrubbing a hand over his face, he checked the clock. After midnight.

Maybe it was Sebastian. A problem with the

horses maybe. Dragging on some jeans, he stumbled barefoot down the stairs. Bo and Peep danced in the entryway, whining and crying.

"Calm down," he rasped, flipping on the front porch light and reaching for the door.

Athena stood on the other side.

For half a second, Logan wondered if he was still dreaming. If he'd summoned her out of sheer want. The rough bump of the dogs shoving past him assured him he was conscious. Given how they'd parted, she was the last person he expected to see on his doorstep. In the seconds his brain took to register that she was really here, Bo and Peep swarmed her, headbutting her legs, yipping delighted greetings.

She crouched enough to love on them, but didn't take her eyes from his face. "I woke you. I'm sorry. I drove straight here from the airport."

Her expression was guarded, and every line of her body shouted anxiety.

About seeing him? About something else?

Whatever it was, he wanted to gather her in his arms and make it better. But that would be pretending their fight hadn't happened. That nothing had changed.

Instead, he stepped back. "It's fine. Come in. I didn't expect you back so soon." As his brain began to fire, he realized she shouldn't have been back before the end of the week. He woke the rest of the way up in a flash. "Is everything all right? Your dad? Your sisters?"

Straightening from the dogs, she moved past him into the house. "Dad's fine so far as I know. I haven't talked to anybody but Maggie to say I was coming home early."

Home.

He wanted to read significance into that but didn't dare let himself hope. Instead, he shut the door and waited, trailing her into the living room, flipping on lights. Did it mean something that she hadn't chosen the kitchen?

She dropped into one of the chairs, tangling her hands and sucking in a long breath as she

319

looked at the floor. "My meeting with the network execs was this morning."

Logan didn't even breathe as he sat on the adjacent sofa and braced himself for whatever came next.

Athena heaved another huge sigh. "You were right."

There was no relief in that, no vindication. Not when she sat there, shoulders slumped in defeat.

"I'm sorry." And he was. He knew how badly she needed to know what came next, needed to have a plan for moving forward.

"They wanted to make a spectacle of me. Turn me into the female Gordon Ramsay. Play up on the notoriety I established in that viral video."

Temper and indignation stirred on her behalf. That was even worse than he'd imagined, and it would've been like a kick to the ribs for her already wounded pride. "Assholes."

A burst of sound that might've been a laugh escaped her. "Yeah. I walked out in the middle of the meeting." She lifted her gaze to his and her eyes were fierce. "I wasn't that desperate."

He winced. "I'm sorry for what I said."

She shook her head. "You're not. Not when you were mostly right."

She had him there. "Then I'm sorry for how I said it. Which part did I get wrong?"

"That I didn't want to walk away from that life. I had already made that decision. But I want to do it on my terms. That's what I hoped to get out of this show. Not a long-term career change. A chance to walk away on a positive note."

"Would it piss you off if I said I'd more or less figured that out?"

"No, I don't think it would. Not now."

And what does that mean? "It was after you left. Or after I stuck my foot in it, and you left, and I wallowed, and drank a bit, and wallowed. And then I realized I didn't give you a chance to say any of that because I was too busy shoving my opinion down your throat." Now it was his turn to sigh. "And panicking about the idea that you were leaving. It was not my best moment."

"I'm not a big fan of anybody who says anything is for my own good."

"Is that what you meant when you said I'd been using my skills to try to handle you?"

She folded both arms across her middle. "I don't have a good history with therapists. It was school counselors and social workers and well-intentioned teachers that I trusted, who questioned me and used my answers to take me away from my father. There was a whole lot of stuff done for my own good, with no thought to what I wanted, because they had their own agendas."

"My only agenda was to protect you."

Restless energy pumped off her in waves. She shoved to her feet and began to pace. "I know. You said it because you care."

Care. Such a pale word for what he felt for her, but she was clearly working up to something, so he stayed quiet.

"You're not like them. Even when you were

yelling at me, you were still doing it because you cared. You didn't betray me, and it wasn't fair of me to lump you in with the people who did." She made a tight circuit of the room. "I thought a lot about that on the flight home. I'm not used to anybody looking out for me."

"Your sisters—"

Athena waved a dismissive hand. "Yes, of course, them, but they know the limits of what I'll tolerate. Which isn't much. I've been on my own for a very, very long time, and the truth is, I haven't trusted anybody enough to let them try to protect me or take care of me since my dad's overdose. Joan did, to a point. But it's not the same. I didn't—couldn't—trust anybody all the way because the one person I should've been able to count on let me down. It's really hard for me to admit that out loud. Because it feels like a betrayal of my dad somehow." She shot a glance in his direction as if daring him to say she was right. "He did the best he could."

A dozen responses scrolled through Logan's head, but all of them were either profane or clinical, neither of which would serve him here. "It still left you in a bad spot. You're allowed to feel about that however you feel. You were a kid." It still infuriated him to imagine what she'd gone through. What she'd been forced to confront at so young an age.

"I was a kid," she agreed. "And I got left alone because he felt backed into a corner, like he had no other choices. He made the one in front of him, and it was the wrong one. I don't want to do that. I don't want to make a choice in the name of taking care of him that's going to leave me alone again. I don't want to leave my family." She stopped pacing to face him. "I don't want to leave you."

Relief hit him fast and hard, stealing his breath. It wasn't a permanent answer, not yet, but it was an admission she wanted to find one. That was enough for now. Reaching out, Logan snagged her hand and tugged her down to his lap. All his rough edges smoothed out as she leaned in, wrapping her arms around him. Skimming a hand through her hair, he pressed his brow to hers. "Well that's handy. Because I'm in love with you."

She jerked back far enough to look into his face, eyes wide. "Logan."

"No pressure. Just fact. I think I was more than halfway there last summer."

"I—"

"You don't have to say anything back. I just wanted you to factor that in as we're figuring out what comes next."

"Will you please shut up a minute?"

He lifted his brows at the snap in her tone. "Yes, ma'am. Do you know I can't resist when you say please?"

She gave him a look. "Then please, hush. I left my meeting, took a cab back to Maggie's to grab my stuff, and went straight to the airport, where I took three flights to get back to Nashville and drove straight here in the middle of the damned night because I couldn't wait another day to fix things with you."

His lips twitched. "You could've called."

Exasperated, she thumped him on the

shoulder. "I was not going to tell you I love you over the damned phone."

Surprise and wonder stole his breath. Or maybe that was just her. He hadn't expected this, not this soon. All the jumbled, broken pieces she'd left in her wake when she walked out fell back into place, and his world felt right again. But he couldn't resist teasing her. "No?"

"You can't have makeup sex over the phone."

"That is a true thing." He stroked a hand down her spine. "Does that mean we're made up now?"

"We're not naked yet."

"Shall we see what we can do about that?"

"Yes, please."

Athena had come braced for a fight. For rejection. For a really obnoxious I told you so. But Logan didn't do any of that. Because that wasn't who he was. Thank God.

So why wasn't she already kissing him?

Sensing her hesitation, Logan skimmed a hand up her spine. "Did we forget something?"

"No. I just…this feels different."

"Different bad?"

"Different huge. Different scary." How could she explain to him that this was like taking her first steps in a whole new body because she was…someone other than she'd always been.

"I'm right here with you. No more facing the scary stuff alone."

Could she really do that? She'd been her own protector for longer than she could remember. Could she really trust him with this?

He drew her in and laid his lips over hers. They both sighed, and she felt his coiled muscles ease, as if he'd suffered as much as she had the last couple of days. Probably he had. He was in love with her, after all. And that was a freaking miracle. Logan Maxwell was in love with her, in spite of—or maybe because of who she was. Difficult, frustrating, and stubborn. As much of a challenge as the land he'd made his own. There was probably something poetic in that. And that was exactly the reason she could and would trust him with her heart.

She framed his face in her hands, loving the rasp of his beard against her palms. "Just thinking how very lucky I am." On a sigh, she brushed her lips back to his. "I love you, Logan." It was terrifying and thrilling to admit it. "I've never said that to any other guy."

A shudder went through him, and his hands tightened on her. After another moment's hesitation, he skimmed his lips along her jaw, down the column of her throat. "I figured on taking another few months to convince you of that."

"Oh?" The word was part question part exclamation as her head dropped back to give him better access.

His path continued from her collar bone, back up to the shell of her ear, igniting little fires in his wake. "Yeah, I had this whole plan not to rush you, to make myself indispensable, until you figured out you couldn't live without me. I'm really good at waiting."

As gooseflesh pebbled along her skin, she

threaded fingers in his hair. "I'm really not. Take me upstairs."

She felt his smile against her skin as he slid an arm under her legs and scooped her up, bride-style. Sensing a game, Bo and Peep leapt to their feet, all wags.

"Stay," Logan ordered.

Peep whined. Bo took two, prancing steps toward the stairs.

"I'll make you something awesome in the morning," Athena promised.

They trailed up the stairs anyway, huffing in insult when Logan kicked the bedroom door shut in their faces.

"Poor babies," Athena murmured.

"They'll get over it," Logan promised, laying her out on the bed and stretching out over her.

She wrapped around him, trailing her hands down the smooth, warm skin of his back and sliding them into his jeans. He wasn't wearing any boxers.

"Somebody surprised me out of bed."

Giving his taut ass a squeeze, she lifted her

mouth to nibble along his throat. "Sorry. Not sorry."

"We'll both be very not sorry by the time we're finished."

His promise had a rush of heat blooming in her core. "I do love that you're a man of your word."

She thought he'd rush. Strip her down and plunge into her, wiping away the distance that had built between them. She loved making him break his control, loved seeing that patience he so prized stripped away by wanting her. But tonight his stubborn outmatched hers.

He took his time, slowly nudging up her shirt, stroking, tracing every newly exposed inch. By the time he finally pulled it off, her skin was humming with desire. She wanted to feel his hands on her, his weight. Thinking to speed things up, she reached for the waistband of his jeans, but he neatly dodged her, pinning her hands and fastening his mouth on one nipple to suckle over her bra.

"Logan." His name was a plea and a protest. "I need more."

"You'll have more. On my schedule this time."

With one hand, he released the clasp of her bra and drew it away. Her breasts spilled free, into the warmth of his callused hands, and she moaned, arching into his touch. He settled one denim-clad leg between her thighs, against her core, and she lifted her hips to rub against him. The warm rasp of his tongue sent bolts of pleasure straight from her tightened nipples down to her center. Cupping his head, she whimpered and rolled against him to the rhythm of his mouth.

Reaching between them, he flicked open the button of her jeans, easing the zipper down.

"Yes. Dear God, yes. I need to be naked. I need to feel you."

But instead of tugging off her jeans, he slid a hand beneath her panties, cupping the warmth of her sex. The pressure of skin against her most sensitive places made up for the disappointment, and she opened her legs wide in invitation. Still worshiping her breast, he curled a finger inside her. She cried out with the pleasure of it, rolling her hips against the heel of his hand. He slid a second finger into her, stretching her, filling her and she rode him, lost to everything but the demands he made on her body, until she shot over the hard, brutal edge, shouting his name.

He eased her down with his lips, his hands, paying homage to her hips and legs as he dragged off the rest of her clothes.

With eyes heavy from release, she watched him, still in his jeans. "No fair. My arms don't work right now."

His grin was smug. "I've got this." He stripped them off, kicking them to the floor and rolling back to her. Finally, skin against glorious skin.

She pressed her face against his throat, inhaling the scent of him—something like leather and leaves and Logan. Home. "I love you."

Her quiet words had the effect her demands

had not, stripping away some of his patience. Reaching for the bedside drawer, he found a condom, rolled it on. Then he was over her, his weight pressing her into the mattress, his erection nudging her center as he curved a hand around her cheek. "Athena. My beautiful, brave Athena."

Turning her face into his palm, she whispered, "Yes." She was his. Completely, happily his.

"I love you." He took her mouth as he took her body, with exquisite care and maddening slowness.

This time, when he filled her, it was more than what they'd had before, as he'd become more. He'd become all. And as they neared the end of that glorious climb, as pleasure stoked pleasure and lit up every dark place inside her, she thought nothing would ever feel as wonderful as making love with this man. Except maybe doing it all over again for the rest of forever.

After they'd thoroughly wrecked each other,

when they lay in panting silence, hearts still thundering, Athena tucked her head against his shoulder. "You were right."

"About what?" he wheezed.

"Definitely not sorry."

On a laugh, he curled his arm tighter around her waist and pressed a kiss to her temple. "No. I'll never be sorry for this. Will you stay tonight?"

"Even if you hadn't completely robbed me of motor function."

She felt his whole body smile against her. "You're onto my evil plan."

"Does your evil plan involve doing that again in the morning to make up for your bastard rooster?"

"I believe that can be arranged."

"Then you'll need a crowbar to get me out of your bed."

"Definitely no crowbar needed."

Kissing her again, he made a quick trip to the bathroom to take care of necessities, before crawling back in and wrapping around her. "Get some sleep, baby."

Exhausted, satisfied, she relaxed against him, loving the feel of his body going lax against hers. But she couldn't settle. It felt almost like those nights when everything had gone right in her kitchen, when she felt like the queen of her world, and her mind wouldn't stop racing from the high. Except this time she was thinking of Logan and the pieces of their very different lives. How she could make them mesh. She'd figure it out. She had faith in that now. But she didn't have the details worked out yet, so her brain was turning over all the pieces, examining the details.

"Logan?"

"Hmm?"

"Are you busy all day tomorrow?"

Chuckling, he brushed his lips against her nape. "I can delegate most of it in the name of keeping you in my bed."

She snorted. "As appealing an idea as that is,

it's not what I meant. I was hoping you'd go with me to Johnson City."

"For what?"

"To meet my dad."

He went very still. "Xander said you don't even take your sisters to see him."

"I don't." It was too hard to have other people see the state he was in. "But I'd like him to meet you."

He curled tighter around her. "Then we'll go tomorrow afternoon."

Okay, that was a first step. Showing him this piece of her life that no one had ever been allowed to see. The idea of it ought to freak her out. She shared her dad with no one. But finally...finally she felt like she could.

Letting go of a last, lingering tension, she slid off into sleep.

CHAPTER 15

Over the forty-minute drive to Johnson City, Logan watched Athena transform. With every mile closer, she became more resolute, and the fingers holding the pie in her lap tightened. She didn't seem to want to talk, and that was fine. He understood this was a huge deal for her, for them. With no clue how it would go, he wanted to do whatever he could to ease things for her. He couldn't begin to imagine how hard it'd been for her dealing with her father alone all these years.

As they turned through the stone-pillared

entrance of Haven Acres, she sucked in a breath. "I feel like I should say something to prepare you, but I just don't know what. I don't know if it'll be a good day or a bad day. It's been bad days more often than not lately. He may not acknowledge you. He may not even know me." Her usually confident voice was choked with emotion, and Logan understood better than he had before that her father wasn't simply an obligation. He was the heart she so carefully guarded.

Reaching over, Logan laid a hand on her leg. "He'll be how he is, and I'll be right there with you. If you don't get through to him today, maybe next time. I'll be with you then, too. You're not alone in this anymore."

He parked in the small lot to the side of the main building, beneath the shade of a massive oak tree. Athena was out of the car almost before he'd shut it off, not from excitement, but as if she had to keep herself moving or risk not going at all. Hurrying after her, Logan wrapped an arm around her, pressing a kiss to her brow. "Whatever you need."

For just a moment, she leaned into him, then straightened again, squaring her shoulders. As she marched through the front doors, she held the pie like a shield.

"Miss Reynolds! So lovely to see you again." The woman behind the reception desk beamed at her.

"Hey Stacey. Can you tell me where he is at the moment?"

Stacey's fingers flew over the keyboard of her computer as she consulted some kind of schedule. "Library."

Athena blinked. "The library?"

"They've been trying something new with him. Do you know where it is?"

"I remember." Back ramrod straight, shoulders back, she headed down the hall as if she were marching to an execution. The sight of it broke Logan's heart.

At the door to the library, she hesitated, one

hand on the wood. The skin over her cheeks was tight with strain.

Logan stroked a hand down her rigid back. "What is it?"

"I just…it's hard to see him in here."

"In the library? Why?"

Inhaling a shaky breath, she turned from the door to face him. "My father isn't a traditionally educated man. He never got more than a high school diploma. But he firmly believed in educating yourself, in always continuing to learn. We had books all over the house, everything from Plato to Rumi to Tolkien. He loved mythology and fantasy. It's how I got my name."

Being a big reader himself, Logan liked the idea of her dad picking out her name from myth. A big name for the girl who would become an amazing woman. "Sounds like a nice memory."

She swallowed hard. "He hasn't been able to read since the overdose. We read to him, but I don't know how much he really takes in anymore. I just think how much he would've loved this place before and knowing he can't truly enjoy it now, I just…it's unbearably sad."

In contrast to her words, she fixed a smile on her face and pulled open the door. The big room was lined with bookcases that stretched all the way to the top of the vaulted ceiling. Huge picture windows looked out over more of the grounds, and there were groupings of comfortable chairs and couches, tables and chairs. The only patrons seemed to be a man in a wheelchair wearing headphones and a woman who sat knitting beside him. Athena strode straight to them, speaking first to the nurse.

"He so likes being read to, and so enjoys this room, we thought we'd try some audiobooks. The occupational therapist is working with him on being able to work the controls of the player." She leaned over to stop the book and tugged the headphones off.

A faint flicker of something that might have been annoyance crossed the man's otherwise vacant face, but it was hard to tell from this angle. The guy appeared to be in his late fifties, but Logan guessed he was actually younger than that. His mostly gray hair still held strands of the golden brown Athena must've inherited from him.

"Theo, you have a visitor."

Athena set the pie on the table. Her father's gaze followed it, and for a moment she could only stare, the dumbfounded shock on her face telling Logan that this kind of reaction wasn't the usual. Finding her smile again, Athena took the chair across from him.

"Hey Daddy. I brought you a pie. It's peach. Your favorite. I picked the peaches from the orchard at the farm myself this morning."

With great effort, Theo turned his head toward his daughter. There was confusion in his expression, and something else.

When she reached out a trembling hand, Logan took it, stepping in to join her.

"There's somebody I want you to meet. Daddy, this is Logan Maxwell. He bought our farm, and he's done wonderful things with it. He's expanded and planted everything you can imagine. I wish you could see it. It's everything you knew it could be."

"I've got pictures on my phone. If you'd like to see." Belatedly, he wondered if he should've refrained from the offer. Would her father get upset at seeing someone else realize what he couldn't?

But as Theo's unsteady gaze tracked to Logan's, Athena squeezed his hand. They were Athena's eyes, without her sharp mind behind them. Yet her father clearly understood some of what they were saying. Taking that as interest, Logan flipped open his camera roll and pulled a chair up next to her dad.

"These are my dogs, Bo and Peep."

Slowly, he swiped through his collection of pictures, giving Theo a virtual tour of the farm. The fields, the hoop houses, the barns, the horses and other livestock. Theo didn't react to any of them. Maybe this hadn't been a good idea.

Logan started to pull the phone away, but Theo's hand jerked, as if reaching out to stop him. Logan looked down to see a selfie of him and Athena, pressed cheek to cheek, grinning on the porch swing on the front of the house.

Logan zoomed in on their faces and held it so Theo could see better. "She looks happy doesn't she?"

Her dad's breathing got heavier.

Praying he was making the right call, Logan continued. "She's a helluva woman, your girl. I'm completely in love with her."

Theo's eyes wheeled toward Athena.

The gray of her eyes was silvered with the sheen of unshed tears, but she lifted the corners of her mouth. "Yeah, I'm in love with him, too."

The nurse, who hadn't left the table, clutched at her chest and sniffed. "Oh, that's so lovely."

"I only just got her to admit it, but I'm working my way toward convincing her to move in with me. To come back home to where her heart never left."

Athena hissed a breath, but Logan kept his attention on her father, willing him to understand. He had no idea how much of his mind was left, but if there was any of the father, he had to carry guilt over what had happened, over what had happened to his daughter because of it. Maybe this was a way of setting things right for both of them.

After an endless minute, Theo's hand lifted, trembling with palsy before it finally landed on Logan's arm. It felt like a victory.

Without hesitation, he covered it with his own hand. "I promise I'll take care of her."

Theo managed a single, shaky nod before his hand fell away.

Silent tears streamed down Athena's cheeks, but when she spoke, her voice was lighter, brighter. "Yeah, so, that's the big news. I'm staying in Eden's Ridge. I haven't exactly figured out how yet, but I'll be around to see you more often."

Her father's gaze shifted toward her again, and Logan could see recognition there. Something she obviously hadn't seen in a long time.

Sucking in a breath, his lips worked until he managed to push out one, clear syllable. "Pie."

Athena laughed through harder tears. "We can totally have some pie."

As soon as they left Haven Acres, Athena called Kennedy. "I need you to gather everybody for a family meeting."

"Sure. Is this to do with the show? How did your meeting go?"

"I'll tell you about it when I get there." She glanced at the clock and did a little math. By the time they got back to the farm and she picked up her car... "I should get there in about an hour."

"Wait, here? You're back?"

So Maggie hadn't blabbed. "I am. Or will be. Just get everybody, okay?"

"I'll do my best. Spouses, too?"

Athena glanced over at Logan. "Yeah. Spouses, too. We'll see you in an hour."

"We?" But she hung up without answering Kennedy's question.

Logan went brows up. "You want me there for a family meeting?"

"It's about helping me find a way to stay. I figured you'd want in on that."

"Hell yeah."

It felt good having him by her side, in knowing she wasn't going into this alone. Weird, but good. She went quiet, thinking about how the visit with her dad had gone. Better than her wildest imaginings. Her father had known her. He'd responded to her. He'd *spoken* for the first time in years. It wasn't nearly enough, but it was so much more than she'd had for far too long. All because of Logan. Because of the farm. Because he'd promised to take care of her. Because he loved her.

"Did you mean it?"

Logan glanced over from the driver's seat. "Mean what?"

"What you said to Daddy about me moving in with you."

"That is the next step, as far as I'm concerned. You love the farm. You love me. Why not come home?"

Athena closed her eyes against overwhelming emotion. He couldn't possibly know how huge this was for her. It was the one thing she couldn't work toward, couldn't earn herself. The one thing she'd wanted more than anything else for the past fourteen years. And here he was offering it freely. A part of her wanted to jump. Wanted to go back to Chicago, pack up all her stuff, and move right on in to make a life with him. And yet...

"I want to come home. You can't know how much. But we're so new, Logan, and I don't want to make a hasty decision colored by you giving me the one thing absolutely no one else possibly could."

His lips curved up into a smile as he grabbed her hand. "That's why I haven't asked you yet. You're not ready. Now you've got plenty of time to get used to the idea, so when I do ask, you'll have an answer." He pressed a kiss to her knuckles. "One thing at a time. Right now, let's sort out the details for how you get to stay."

For the rest of the drive, she turned over the details in her head, but it was just more looking at pieces that didn't seem to fit. Coming home wasn't going to be smooth or easy. Maybe that was because she was one of those pieces that didn't fit. In some ways she never had. But that was the beauty of the home she'd been given. The Misfit Inn had been a home for misfit kids long before she and her sisters had turned it into an inn. Somehow Joan had always known the right way to reach each and every one. To make those differences things to be celebrated. She'd always encouraged her kids to build their place, and so Athena had. Far away from here. She'd made a name for herself. But as the sprawling Victorian came into view and she thought of the family waiting for her inside, she decided she was tired of trying to build a name. She was ready to build a life.

Logan met her at the bottom of the steps. "You ready?"

She slid her hand into his and felt at least one of those pieces clicking into place. "Absolutely."

The sound of voices drew them back to the kitchen.

"You're back early!" Ari flew across the room, wrapping Athena in a tight hug. "Does this mean L.A. was terrible and you're not moving?"

Trust the kid to zero in on the heart of the matter. "Not to put too fine a point on it, but yes."

Ari whooped and pumped her fist.

"Ari, that might not be good news to Athena," Pru pointed out.

The girl's cheeks colored. "Sorry."

"It's fine. I mean, I'm disappointed. I liked the idea of a show, but it wasn't the right fit. Somebody get Maggie on the line."

As Flynn set up the iPad for teleconferencing at the kitchen table, Athena moved around the room, giving and receiving hugs from her sisters and her brothers-in-law. And if she held on a little longer than she would have in the past, no one remarked on it. There were a few raised eyebrows at Logan's presence, particularly when Athena pulled him down beside her at the table, but for the moment, everyone seemed content to wait for her explanation.

Maggie's face filled the screen. "Well, I'm glad to see you got back okay last night."

"Last night?" Pru asked.

Athena leaned into the arm Logan wrapped around her. "I got back late and had some business to tend to."

"Is that what they're calling it these days?" Xander huffed a laugh as Kennedy drove an elbow into his gut.

"So that got fixed," Pru concluded. "Good."

"You know, I knew as soon as you got out here that you weren't going to stay in L.A." Maggie's attention shifted to Logan. "Much as I wanted family close by, I was pulling for you. You're good for her."

"Thanks."

Athena hated being talked about as if she wasn't in the room. "I'm right here, y'all."

Logan pressed a kiss to her temple. "Then take the floor."

"Okay, so I don't much feel like getting into the nitty gritty about my meeting with the producers at SizzleTV. Let's just say we did not come to an agreement on our visions for the show and leave it at that." She'd love to leave that whole experience in the past, never to be thought of again. "The point of this meeting is to brainstorm. I want to stay here. Not just as a temporary stopover until I figure out what's next. I want to come home for real. I need a viable way to do it that still allows me to financially take care of my dad."

Everybody started talking at once and the immediate outpouring of enthusiasm made Athena's eyes burn. She'd had enough with crying today, even for good reasons, but it was so wonderful to feel her family's support.

Logan's calm, matter-of-fact voice cut

through the noise. "Okay, everybody slow down."

"I still think the most obvious and practical answer is to open a restaurant as part of the inn," Pru said.

Of course the ready answer was to bring her in as part of the family business. A part of her liked the idea of it, of being a part of something greater. She'd spent a long time running her own ship. But none of this was as simple as they thought it was.

"That might be something to think about down the line, but right now the concept should be tabled." At the chorus of buts that sounded, Athena lifted a hand. "Opening a restaurant, even a small scale one, is extremely expensive and right now there's simply not the money to support it. Profits are being funneled into the second phase expansion for the spa, and that's as it should be. I'm not saying never, but that's not a decision I could make fast or lightly. Eden's Ridge is a town of less than three thousand people. Even with tourism, I don't know that there's an adequate market to justify the expense."

"What about the cooking school?" Ari asked. "That went really well, and you enjoyed it. Well, except for the asshat." At her mother's bland stare, she shrugged. "Well he was."

"I like the cooking school better. I truly did enjoy teaching. But I don't think I could sustain that scale all the time. By the end of that four week stretch, I was peopled out."

"So do a smaller scale," Xander urged.

"There comes a point of diminishing returns. It's one thing to do a short run of something out of the diner, but that's not practical for creating an actual business. To do a cooking school right, it would have to be more than one day a week, and would need its own space. Something would have to be leased or built or bought, then furnished with multiple sets of tools and appliances, all of which cost more money than I'm afraid we have right now and would require a higher student enrollment than I think I could stand."

Ari started to speak again but Kennedy jumped in.

"What about catering?"

Athena shuddered. "It's…not at the top of my list. But I'm not in a financial position to be a snob about it. It's something I can do with the facilities we have. I did it to make extra money while I was in culinary school. It might be something I could do for the short-term to start saving toward one of the other options." And that might be how she'd have to approach this. Cobbling together a lot of different things to save up for something longer term. Once she figured out what that would be, anyway.

"Good. Because I've got another idea." Kennedy leaned forward. "My book launch is coming up week after next. My editor is going to be in town. When I told her you were here, she might have casually mentioned the advances for some higher profile cookbooks lately and said that her colleague is still interested."

Athena dimly remembered that conversation with Elena Beckhoff at the inn's opening last year. She'd shrugged it off at the time, too focused on Olympus to consider it. But now? "What kind of advances?"

Kennedy named several figures that had Athena's interest sparking anew.

"An advance like that would give me enough to cover several more months at Haven Acres for Daddy."

"I mean, no guarantees obviously, but it seems worth a shot if you're interested," Kennedy said. "And with a cookbook, you'd put together a proposal for what you want to do, so it's not like the SizzleTV thing where you were going in mostly blind."

"I like the idea of a cookbook. It's a project I'd enjoy. One that wouldn't require enormous amounts of peopling." And while it would certainly require input from a team, it wouldn't be like the train wreck of a show. A cookbook would inherently be about the food. "Yeah, I'd like to talk to Elena's colleague if they're still interested."

Kennedy grinned. "Well, obviously you'll cater the affair to knock Elena's socks off to send good word back to New York. And I'll help you put together a proposal."

Feeling as if she at least had a direction, Athena grabbed a notebook from the counter. "Let's talk menu."

ATHENA PACED a tight circle around the island in the inn's kitchen, mentally reviewing her lists. The charcuterie trays were finished. The cheese boards were loaded. The crudités were laid out in a rainbow of foodie perfection. Every public room on the lower floor of the inn was set up with elegantly-appointed food tables that represented the different regions highlighted in Kennedy's book. A culinary journey for the guests of the travel writer. If they ever freaking arrived.

She started to check the clock again just as Logan appeared in the doorway.

"Relax. Everything's set. And it looks and smells amazing."

When he crossed over, cupping her elbows to draw her closer, she snuggled in, reveling in his solid, steady warmth. "I just want everything to be perfect."

"It is. You are."

Lifting her head from his chest, she fixed him with a bland stare. "That seems a stretch."

His lips quirked into a smile. "Well, perfect for me." His mouth was a hairsbreadth from hers when they heard the front door open and Kennedy squealing, "You made it!"

Athena jolted. "They're here!" Jerking away from him, she brushed at the front of her apron. "How do I look?"

"Gorgeous and a little crazed."

Glaring, she yanked the apron off and made a beeline for the foyer.

But it wasn't Kennedy's editor. It was Maggie.

"You're here! I didn't think you were going

to be able to make it." Athena grabbed her sister up in a hug.

"I'm literally only here until tomorrow. But I wouldn't have missed this for the world."

"Maggie!" Pru shuffled in from the office.

Maggie wrapped her in a careful hug. "How's the little mama?"

Pru laughed. "Not so little anymore." She rubbed a hand over the swell of her belly and winced. "I swear, this baby has set up camp on my bladder. Be back."

As she disappeared, Porter emerged from the guest lounge, a bacon-wrapped fig in his hand. "Hey, these are amazing."

"You aren't supposed to touch those until the guests arrive!" Athena snapped.

Unruffled, he only smiled and popped the fig into his mouth. "I am a guest." Turning to Maggie, his smile morphed into something softer and a little sadder. "Hey Maggie. Can I carry your bag upstairs for you so you can visit with your sisters?"

"That'd be great. Thanks, Porter." Utterly oblivious, she passed off her carry-on.

With one last look full of something that might have been regret, he disappeared upstairs.

Not my business, Athena reminded herself. That whole situation was too many years in the making for her to interfere now. She had too much of her own stuff to deal with, struggling not to get her hopes up. A cookbook might not work out and even if it did, publishing took time.

Focus on what's in front of you.

Maggie skimmed her hands over Athena's shoulders. "You ready?"

"It's Kennedy's night." It felt stupid and selfish to be so focused on what it could mean for her.

Kennedy slid an arm around Athena's waist. "Hey, I already went through the hard part. We're celebrating my book launch, sure, but this is as much about showing you off."

She appreciated the show of support. "I guess I'm as ready as I'm going to be."

"You finished the cookbook proposal," Kennedy reminded her.

"Your definition of finished and mine are clearly not the same." She'd have preferred another month to play and perfect and polish.

"Perfectionist. This is fine. It's a sampling meant to whet the appetite just as much as your food."

"I'd feel a lot more confident if Elena's colleague was going to be here to *eat* my food."

In the momentary silence, they all heard car doors closing.

Kennedy grinned. "Yeah, about that."

Athena swung to look at her sister as Flynn went to answer the door. "What are you talking about?"

"Elena's not alone."

"Oh my God." Athena's shock got lost in the flurry of people coming into the house.

"Welcome to the Misfit Inn." Flynn's cheerful welcome presaged the arrival of a quartet of women whose polished looks proclaimed *Not From Around Here.*

Logan's arm slid around her waist. "You've got this," he murmured.

Athena wasn't at all sure she did. Not since her initial meeting with prospective investors for Olympus had she been this nervous. She only half heard introductions to Kennedy's agent, Taryn Whitney, and her publicist Keely Booker who'd come along for the fun.

"And this is my colleague, Yasmine Fenton. Yasmine's the one I was telling you about," Elena explained.

Kennedy shook hands and beamed. "It's so nice to meet you. Please allow me to introduce you to my family." She made the rounds, listing off more names than the woman could possibly remember, before finally laying a hand on Athena's shoulder. "And this is my brilliant and talented award-winning sister, Chef Athena Reynolds."

Oh my God. What if she's seen the video? What if she heard about my lost star? What if—

Yasmine extended a hand. "I'm very pleased to meet you, Chef Reynolds."

Numb, Athena shook it. "I'm sorry, I only speak food when I'm nervous. Can I offer you some appetizers?"

Her grin flashed white against flawless roux brown skin. "I'd love some."

Yasmine was gracious and appreciative, striking a good note with Athena as they made the rounds and other guests began to arrive.

"Oh my God, have you tried these pimento cheese beignets? They are *to die for*."

"I know, and the bacon-wrapped figs?"

It pleased her hearing people enjoying her food. Not overanalyzing, not critiquing, just eating and appreciating.

By the time she finished giving Yasmine the tour of food, the house was full of people, laughing and chattering. Several of the appetizers had already been decimated.

"If you'll excuse me, I need to refill these trays."

Needing a minute or five, Athena retreated

to the kitchen and began methodically loading trays from the containers in the fridge. That had gone...as well as it could, she supposed. There'd been no talk of the proposal, but that was fine. It seemed wrong to do a hard sell straight out of the gate. No matter what Kennedy said, this was her night, her triumph to celebrate.

Yasmine wandered in. "I'm sorry to intrude, but I had to see if there were more of those pan-fried ricotta dumplings." Spying the tray Athena was in the middle of refilling, she grabbed another one and bit in. Her dark eyes closed and she gave a low moan of satisfaction. "This is fantastic."

Some of the nerves settled. Athena knew her food made up for any deficiencies in her social skills. "Glad you're enjoying it. It pairs particularly well with the pinot Grigio from Temptation Vineyards."

"I'll definitely try that. And I know you're basically working this party, but later I'd love to discuss the possibility of a cookbook."

Athena briskly wiped her hands on a kitchen towel. "Already?"

"It's why I came down here. Elena's been raving about your food since the inn opened last year. There's no question you can cook. We just need to come up with proof of viability for me to take back with me to New York."

"Actually, I think I've got proof of definite viability."

They both turned as Ari slipped out of the family living room. Of course the kid was eavesdropping again.

"What are you talking about?" Athena asked.

"After the party," she promised. "We'll round up the New York folks and I'll show you." She slipped out of the room.

Staring after her, Athena explained, "That's my niece, Ari. I have no idea what she's cooked up."

Yasmine just smiled, clearly amused. "I guess we'll find out at the end of the night."

Athena intended to find out sooner than that, but her imp of a niece managed to successfully evade being cornered until the food had been demolished and the last guest had been ushered out the door. Athena finally found her head-to-head with Kennedy in the office.

"Ariana Rosas Reynolds Bohannon, what are you up to?"

Ari just angled her head and looked at Kennedy. "Is the middle naming supposed to have the same effect if it comes from someone other than a parent?"

Kennedy snickered. "Come on. Let's round everybody up."

"You're in on this?" Athena demanded.

"I am. Just be patient and we'll explain all."

Athena found herself herded, along with both her sisters and their husbands, Logan, and the contingent from New York, into the family living room. A projector had been set up. Where the hell did that come from? As people settled in chairs and on the sofa or leaned against walls, Ari opened a laptop.

"Okay, so now that we're done with the cel-ebration portion of the evening, I have something else to show you. I think we can all agree that the food tonight was phenomenal."

There were murmurs of agreement.

"I know when y'all head back to New York, you'll be taking a cookbook proposal with you. But there's more to be factored in here than just the awesome food."

"You mentioned viability of concept," Yasmine said.

"So I did. Over the past few months, since Athena's been home, she's been teaching me to cook. I recorded most of those sessions, along with the classes she taught in conjunction with Maxwell Organics."

Athena had known Ari had recorded things, but she'd said it was just for posterity, for her own reminders. Where was she going with this? As fresh tension coiled low in her belly, Logan stepped up behind her, pressing a hand to the small of her back. She leaned into him, wishing her knees didn't feel so weak.

"She's a heck of a good teacher, and she could totally do her own show. So Kennedy and

I did some editing of those videos to create a pilot web series."

Oh shit. What has she done?

Ari kept her eyes fixed on the laptop as her fingers flew over the keys. "I give you The Misfit Kitchen."

A website opened, slick and clean, with a picture of Athena laughing in the inn's kitchen front and center. Ari took them through it, clicking on About the Chef, showing some of the videos that had been edited down for a shorter web format. There was a classroom portal and a signup for people interested in in-person classes. "It can be expanded in a lot of different directions. There's even space to attach a food blog, if that's something you're interested in."

Not knowing what else to say, Athena asked, "How does this prove viability of concept?"

"The whole thing is monetized and subscription based, and there's already been an overwhelmingly positive response," Kennedy explained.

"Wait, it's *live?* People are actually subscribing?"

"In droves." Kennedy took over the keyboard and pulled up some other page with charts and numbers that meant absolute bupkis to Athena.

"How? This couldn't have been up all that long."

"Celeste helped, and I put together a social media campaign to get things off the ground. It's not too shabby, if I do say so myself." Kennedy looked a little smug.

"Those are some impressive numbers," Yasmine agreed.

"I don't know what to say," Athena murmured.

Across the room, Ari knit her fingers together, clearly thinking Athena would be mad. "We thought it would be a good way to give you back control."

They'd put her online without her consent. How did that give her back control?

Kennedy picked up the thread. "Web series

are a big thing. If you decide to go with this, it can be done with minimal budget, dialed up or down as time and money allows. You'd retain full creative control and could teach exactly what you want. You're in the driver's seat. Over time, it would create a massive online presence to promote whatever endeavor you choose to pursue, whether that's small-scale private cooking classes, a restaurant, a cookbook, or some combination of all of that."

Anxiety began to recede, replaced with something that might've been excitement. With this she *could* do a cooking show focused legitimately on the food. She could teach the farm-to-table concepts she was so passionate about to a larger audience *without* having to deal with them directly. Every episode would help to create an online presence that would eventually overshadow the infamous video.

"Well, what do you think?" Kennedy demanded.

"The pair of you are nosy, interfering busybodies who clearly subscribe to the school of it's better to ask forgiveness than permission."

Ari cringed.

"And you're both geniuses." Athena crossed the room to pull them both into a fierce group hug. "Thank you."

"You're not mad?" Ari whispered.

"I'm not mad. You're awesome." She tipped her head to Kennedy's. "You're both awesome."

Elena nudged Yasmine. "I told you this family was a publicist's dream to work with."

"It definitely gives me plenty of fodder to play with when I pitch it to acquisitions. Athena, let's talk concepts."

Grinning with relief, Athena picked up a glass of wine and clinked it to Yasmine's. "I would love that."

EPILOGUE

ilming in Progress.

Logan hesitated at the sign on his front door. He'd expected her to be done by now, but maybe he'd had a bit of a lead foot all the way back from Nashville. As the dogs weren't milling around, waiting to slide past him, he took a chance and quietly slipped inside. Shrugging out of his jacket, he hung it on a peg by the door and followed the sound of voices.

Athena stood at the island, her hair up in one of those messy twists as she tipped a casserole dish toward the camera. "Isn't that gorgeous?"

She sure as hell is. Smiling to himself, Logan leaned in the doorway and took her in. Those wide gray eyes were sparkling and that smart mouth he loved so much curved in a broad, easy smile. Happiness practically radiated off her. And why shouldn't it? With the help of her sisters, she'd managed to carve out a niche for herself doing exactly what she wanted—highlighting the farm-to-table cooking she was so passionate about.

The Misfit Kitchen web series and the accompanying food blog had been a runaway success in the past four months, hitting enough subscribers by the beginning of October to effectively cover her dad's care and solidifying the cookbook deal with Yasmine's publishing house. Maggie's growth projections had convinced her it was worth investing more in the show by building a dedicated facility that could be used not only for filming but for hosting cooking retreats in conjunction with the inn.

She even had a call scheduled later this week with a cookware company to discuss corporate sponsorship. All in all, everything was coming up roses. Athena had buried that viral video in good press and earned back her good name *her* way.

She was settled and happy. To Logan's mind, that meant it was time. He slid a hand into his pocket to finger the box that had been burning a hole all through his deliveries and the meetings with two new restaurant clients. He'd been patient. He'd given her time. He was beyond ready to take this next step, and he was counting on her being ready, too.

"That's all the time we've got today, and this will be our last episode this season. But tune in next week anyway, as I'll be giving a quick tour of how the brand new Misfit Kitchen facility is coming along. If all continues to go according to schedule, we'll be filming next there just in time for the new year. *And* I'll be having a special guest chef coming to join me. Moses Lindsey is one of *the best* pastry chefs I've ever had the pleasure of working with, and he's coming down to do a weekend workshop. Links to signup for that are on our website." She aimed a blinding smile at the camera. "Until next year, I'm Chef Athena Reynolds, wishing you and yours a very Merry Christmas."

"And cut!" Scott Barker, the cameraman and one half of Athena's two-person crew, straightened. "That was fabulous. I think we got it all in one take."

"Thank God." Athena rolled her head and unclipped her mic pack before making a beeline in his direction. "You're back!"

"I am." Logan took her mouth in a lingering hello kiss. "Mmm. You smell like rosemary and cream."

Her arms linked around his neck. "Rosemary au gratin potatoes. Hope you like them because that's part of what we're having for dinner."

"I am not opposed to a trial run of Christmas dinner. Though it feels weird to have the kitchen decorated for the occasion when there's still a jack o'lantern on the front porch."

"We'll take them down," Ari promised.

"It's good to have the season in the can early," Scott said. "Plenty of time to edit and fix any errors and upload."

"My minions speak the truth. Plus, it gives me the next couple of months to work on recipes for the cookbook. Yasmine wants a finalized list by the end of January."

"Then let it be so."

Athena slipped away to grab a bottle of water from the fridge. "How did your meetings go?"

"They both signed on the dotted line as brand-new Maxwell Organics clients." Two more to add to the roster that had grown by leaps and bounds since the summer. "Really today was just a formality. They made up their minds after the tour."

One of Athena's ideas had been to set up an overnight visit and tour of the farm in conjunction with the inn for chefs and restaurateurs. So far it had resulted in more than a half dozen new contracts with Nashville and Knoxville area restaurants thanks to Athena's encouragement and the contacts she'd cultivated once she reached out to the foodie scene in the southeast. He'd just about maxed out what they could provide, at least until Porter finished building the new greenhouse. But that would be after he finished the official Misfit Kitchen.

"Woo! I'd say that's something worth opening a fresh bottle of wine to toast."

They'd have more than that to toast before the night was over if he had his way. "I picked a few options up while I was in Nashville."

"We'll figure out what goes best with this balsamic-glazed pork loin. You two are gonna take some of this home with you, right?" Athena looked at her crew.

"Do I ever turn down food?" Scott asked.

"You do not. It has been rumored you have a hollow leg." Ari teased with a grin at the early twenty-something Scott that made Logan wonder if he needed to have a word with Flynn. "It's the best part of this gig."

"Let's get final pictures for the blog post and clean everything up so y'all can get out of here," Athena urged. "Scott, you're still good to drop Ari at home?"

"Sure thing."

Logan pitched in, as much out of habit as a desire to hurry them on their way so he could get Athena alone. Since Pru and Flynn's baby had been born in September, filming had moved to the farm's kitchen. Athena had been spending more nights here herself, claiming that Rudy was less sleep confused than the newest member of the Reynolds family. Logan wasn't about to complain.

By the time they'd broken down all the lights, coiled all the cables, and stowed the rest of the gear, Athena had packaged up part of the demo meal to send home with Scott and Ari.

"I'll edit this latest video and have something for you to proof in a few days," Scott promised.

"Take your time. I know you and Celeste have got that big Christmas project coming up for the Chamber of Commerce."

"Gonna be a stunner for sure. You ready, kid?"

A flicker of irritation crossed Ari's face before she fixed her smile firmly in place. The last thing she wanted was to be seen as a kid. "Sure. Let's go."

Logan watched the pair of them leave, ribbing each other. As soon as they were out of earshot, he turned to Athena. "Do we need to worry about that?"

"Nah. He's her first real crush. She's fifteen. He's twenty-two and doesn't see her as anything other than a little sister. Hence the 'kid' she got so annoyed about. Plus, he's got a thing for Crystal's daughter Nicky."

When he only grunted, she laughed. "Stand down, Papa Bear. I already warned Pru and Flynn. Pru's had a conversation with her, which both of them found utterly mortifying. Scott's a

379

safe one for her to practice her flirting on because it will never go anywhere."

"I suppose that's better than one of her classmates."

"That poor kid had no idea she'd be taking on multiple over-protective parent figures when she got adopted into this family."

"She loves all of us," Logan protested.

"That she does. C'mon. Are you ready to eat now or do you want to wait for later?"

"Let's wait a bit. How about a little walk before dinner? We've got time to catch the sunset."

"Sounds like a plan."

They grabbed light jackets and headed out into the fading light. Bo and Peep raced over from the stables, bumping and barking greetings. After quick, full-body rubs, they seemed content to trot a few yards ahead, sniffing everything as they went. Logan took Athena's hand, loving how she fell into ready step beside him to walk the land that had, in a very real way, brought them together.

Talking of basic, everyday things, they trailed past the stables, beyond Sebastian's little cabin and on up the hill where the ground had been broken for the new greenhouse a couple of weeks back. The framing had been put in place for the foundation and pipes run for irrigation. God and weather willing, the foundation would be poured sometime next week.

"It'll be done before you know it, and then you'll lose the quiet season," Athena observed.

"The quiet season?"

"That's what my dad always used to call winter. There's always something to do on a farm, of course, but winter was always quieter. It's when he used to catch up on reading and make plans for spring. You've got a bigger operation here, but it still slows down in winter, doesn't it?"

"Yeah. The quiet season. I like that. A time to dream and plan for the future." At the top of the hill he stopped and drew her in, resting his cheek on her hair as they looked down over the farm they both loved, gilded by the setting sun.

"Helluva view," she murmured.

"It definitely is. Your dad's gonna enjoy seeing it again when we bring him out next weekend."

"I hope so. He'll never be what he was, but he's made some strides these past few months. There are more good days than there were before, and I think he's gotten to a place where he'll get some peace out of seeing this place."

"It's a good place for finding peace."

They stood, wrapped around each other in the dying light, and Logan bided his time.

When the last rim of sun sank below the horizon, Athena let loose a soft, contented sigh. "I never get tired of seeing that."

Stepping back, Logan kept one of her hands in his. "Ready to go home?"

"Yeah. I think I am."

"Good." Surrounded by the scent of freshly-tilled earth and a watercolor sky, he sank down to one knee.

"Logan." She pressed a hand to her mouth.

"In general, I'm a patient man. I said I'd wait

until you were ready, and I did my best, but it turns out I'm kinda in a hurry. I feel like I've been waiting forever for you. I didn't even know what my life was missing until you came into it. So I hope I've waited long enough for you to adjust to the idea because I want to marry you. I want to bring you back to this land, where you've always belonged, and make a family and life with you. Say you'll be mine, Athena. Say you'll come home to me."

With her free hand, she cupped his cheek. "All I've wanted since I was twelve years old was to come home. It was a dream I gave up a long, long time ago. So to have you giving me that chance, to know that you're part of the package, not for a few days or weeks but a lifetime—well, Farmer Boy, I can't think of anything I want more. So yeah, I'll marry you."

Whooping, Logan shot to his feet, scooping Athena off hers and swinging her in a dizzying circle. The dogs leapt and danced around them, joining in the fun. Laughing, she held on.

"I love you. I love you so damned much."

"Are you gonna show me what's in the box?"

"Oh, right." He set her back down and opened the little box still clutched in his hand. The diamond caught the last faint rays of the sun as he pulled it out and slid it on her left hand.

She ran a thumb over the low profile band. "It's perfect. You're perfect."

"Far from it."

"Perfect for me," she corrected, twining her arms around him and brushing her lips to his in a kiss that was all too brief. "C'mon let's get dinner."

"You want to eat now?"

She tugged away and shot a wicked grin over her shoulder. "You're gonna need your strength to celebrate."

Wrapping an arm around her, he pressed another hard, fast kiss to her mouth. "Yes, Chef."

Choose Your Next Romance

Maggie and Porter's book, *Bring It On Home* is FINALLY available! The final book in The Misfit Inn quartet is a friends-to-lovers romance with secrets aplenty finally revealed. You don't want to miss the return of the final Reynolds sister!

If you'd like a little different flavor, *What I Like About You,* Book 2 in the *Rescue My Heart* trilogy, follows another of that band of brothers, former Army Ranger turned horse trainer Sebastian Donnelly, and Logan's little sister Laurel. Plus, you get to attend Logan and Athena's wedding! Who wants to miss that? Nobody.

OTHER BOOKS BY KAIT NOLAN

A complete and up-to-date list of all my books can be found at https://kaitnolan.com.

THE MISFIT INN SERIES
SMALL TOWN FAMILY ROMANCE

- *When You Got A Good Thing* (Kennedy and Xander)
- *Til There Was You* (Misty and Denver)

- *Those Sweet Words* (Pru and Flynn)
- *Stay A Little Longer* (Athena and Logan)
- *Bring It On Home* (Maggie and Porter)

RESCUE MY HEART SERIES
SMALL TOWN MILITARY ROMANCE

- *Baby It's Cold Outside* (Ivy and Harrison)
- *What I Like About You* (Laurel and Sebastian)
- *Bad Case of Loving You* (Paisley and Ty prequel)
- *Made For Loving You* (Paisley and Ty)

MEN OF THE MISFIT INN
SMALL TOWN SOUTHERN ROMANCE

- *Let It Be Me* (Emerson and Caleb)
- *Our Kind of Love* (Abbey and Kyle)

WISHFUL SERIES

SMALL TOWN SOUTHERN ROMANCE

- *Once Upon A Coffee* (Avery and Dillon)
- *To Get Me To You* (Cam and Norah)
- *Know Me Well* (Liam and Riley)
- *Be Careful, It's My Heart* (Brody and Tyler)
- *Just For This Moment* (Myles and Piper)
- *Wish I Might* (Reed and Cecily)
- *Turn My World Around* (Tucker and Corinne)
- *Dance Me A Dream* (Jace and Tara)
- *See You Again* (Trey and Sandy)
- *The Christmas Fountain* (Chad and Mary Alice)
- *You Were Meant For Me* (Mitch and Tess)
- *A Lot Like Christmas* (Ryan and Hannah)
- *Dancing Away With My Heart* (Zach and Lexi)

WISHING FOR A HERO SERIES (A WISHFUL SPINOFF SERIES)
SMALL TOWN ROMANTIC SUSPENSE

- *Make You Feel My Love* (Judd and Autumn)
- *Watch Over Me* (Nash and Rowan)
- *Can't Take My Eyes Off You* (Ethan and Miranda)
- *Burn For You* (Sean and Delaney)

MEET CUTE ROMANCE
SMALL TOWN SHORT ROMANCE

- *Once Upon A Snow Day*
- *Once Upon A New Year's Eve*
- *Once Upon An Heirloom*
- *Once Upon A Coffee*
- *Once Upon A Campfire*
- *Once Upon A Rescue*

SUMMER CAMP
CONTEMPORARY ROMANCE

- *Once Upon A Campfire*
- *Second Chance Summer*

www.ingramcontent.com/pod-product-compliance
Lightning Source LLC
Chambersburg PA
CBHW060309100726
47907CB00002B/350